another *June* with you

KRISTA NOORMAN

BOOKS by KRISTA NOORMAN

The Truth About Drew
Goodbye, Magnolia
Hello, Forever
Until Then
18 Hours To Us
Another June with You

And we know that all things work together for good to them that love God, to them who are the called according to his purpose.

Romans 8:28 KJV

Chapter 1

June 2011

Never in Shannon's life had she been late for a job. Not once. In fact, she had never been late for anything. But she was definitely going to be late to Chase and Keely's wedding brunch—the first of several events beginning on Wednesday and spanning the three days leading up to their Saturday afternoon nuptials. All of which she had been hired to photograph. If not for her stupid car not starting—*darn battery!*—and this traffic jam on 131 due to some kind of accident in the middle of a construction zone—*stupid drivers!*—she would've been there by now.

The cars ahead of her inched along, and she pulled out her phone and fired off a quick text to Keely, letting her know where she was.

Keely's reply was as laid back as she was. "No worries, Shannon. See you when you get here." But her calm disposition had no effect on Shannon's, which was more on the anxious end of the personality spectrum.

Only ten more car-lengths until the Pearl Street exit. The exhaust from the truck ahead blew in through the open windows making her cough. If only the air conditioner worked on this unseasonably steamy June morning. She leaned forward and used one hand to lift her long raven locks away from her neck while the other unstuck her shirt from her back. She didn't have to see it to know the shirt was covered in streaks of sweat. *Classy.*

A few more feet.

Nine cars.

Eight.

Still moving. Slowly, but surely.

Only four cars ahead of her now. Getting closer. Her left foot tapped on the rubber floor mat. If only there was enough space on the right for her to squeeze around a couple of the vehicles, but she didn't dare try with the police close by for the accident. So she waited impatiently.

Two more car-lengths.

What is that? Something smelled hot. Really hot. Like it was ... burning. At the moment that word crossed her mind, smoke billowed out from under the hood of her car.

"Nooo!" she cried. "Not now!"

The cars in front of her moved. Of course this would happen just as it was her turn to finally take the exit she needed.

She pressed slowly on the accelerator, hoping she would at least make it off the ramp and into a parking lot or something. The car sputtered and came to a complete stop, partially blocking the top of the exit ramp. Of course it did.

Tears burned her eyes. She couldn't believe this was happening.

A car horn blared just as she grabbed her phone, and she jumped, sending the phone flying onto the passenger side floor mat. Vehicles squeezed around her, most coming close to knocking her mirror off. Some people gave her a look of sympathy, while others flung foul language her way or flipped her off.

She buried her face in her hands for a moment then undid her seatbelt and leaned across the car to get her phone. Who should she call first? Her dad? She hated to bother him at work. Duncan? No, Duncan was still in Denver. *Darn it!* Maybe Jamie. Best friends were supposed to be there for you through thick and thin, right? She kicked herself for not adding roadside assistance to her insurance policy.

Reluctantly, she dialed Keely's number.

"Hey, are you almost here?" Keely sounded as cheerful as always.

"I'm still stuck."

"Must have been a bad accident. I hope nobody was seriously hurt."

"I think it was just a fender bender, but my car overheated and is now dead in the middle of the exit ramp."

"Say no more. I'm sending Chase."

"What? No! You can't send your fiancé. It's your wedding brunch." She could hear Keely's muffled voice in the background talking to someone.

"Okay," Keely came back on. "Tell me exactly where you are. We're sending a tow truck to get your car to a shop and the best man to pick you up."

A combination of relief and embarrassment came over her as she gave Keely her location. "Keely, thank you. I'm so sorry about this."

"Oh, Shannon, it's not your fault. These things happen. We'll see you soon."

They hung up, and Shannon closed her eyes and pinched her nose, blocking out the crazies giving her attitude and the smell of burnt coolant seeping into the cabin. With every car that inched by, she held her breath, hoping they'd just drive on.

A rusty pickup truck stopped behind her, and a burly man got out and walked her way.

She braced herself for a scolding.

"Shift it into neutral, doll," he called out to her.

She did as he said, and he proceeded to push her vehicle while she steered it to the shoulder.

"Do you need me to call anyone?" he asked.

"I already did. Thank you so much."

The man nodded and disappeared into his truck, giving a friendly wave as he drove down the exit.

At least she was out of traffic now.

Fifteen minutes later, a shiny, black Lexus pulled up behind her dirty, rusting VW Golf. In her side mirror, she watched a tall blond man in khakis and a turquoise dress shirt emerge from within. *The best man.*

She climbed out of her car, careful to avoid getting hit by the passing vehicles, and pulled the lever to move her seat forward so she could get to her camera bag, which was stashed on the floor in the back.

"Shannon?" The man's voice had a familiarity to it, and his tone was not that of a stranger asking if she *was* Shannon, but that of a man who was surprised to see someone he knew.

She peered over her shoulder as she lifted her bag. Her stomach somersaulted as he removed his sunglasses and their eyes met. Her bag slipped through her fingers, returning to the floor with a thud.

"Micah." Her voice came out high-pitched and not at all normal.

"Are you the wedding photographer?" He hung the sunglasses from the neck of his shirt.

"I ... yeah, I am. You're ... the best man?" She was a stuttering fool.

He nodded. "I introduced them."

"Oh." She needed to grab her bag, but stood frozen in place, staring at him in disbelief.

"It's been a long time." His eyes were as chocolaty brown as she remembered, like she could melt into them.

She shook herself out of that line of thought. "Yeah. What, like ten years?"

His jaw twitched the way it always had when something bothered him. She couldn't believe she remembered that little detail after all this time.

"Something like that," he replied tersely.

Ten years since they had said goodbye.

Micah Shaw. She couldn't believe he was standing in front of her again. Much less on the side of a highway off-ramp, waiting for her old hunk o' junk to be towed.

"Let me help you with your things. We can wait in my car so we don't melt out here."

His smile made her weak in the knees. But that was nothing new. She'd always reacted strongly to him—his looks, his touch, his kiss.

He moved carefully around her and reached in for her bag.

"Thanks." She tried to ignore the way the muscle in his arm flexed under his shirt. It was obvious he had kept in shape over the years—maybe he still played baseball. She wondered so many things about him, things she'd tried not to let herself think about over the years. First and foremost, was he married? The last she'd heard of him through the grapevine was that he had met someone—someone he was serious about—and was planning to propose. That was more than a year ago, though. And he wasn't wearing a wedding ring. Not yet, anyway.

Shannon followed Micah to the Lexus and climbed into the passenger seat. She glanced around at the smooth leather interior, and a musky cologne wafted her way as he slid in and started the car.

A blast of cold air hit her. "Oh, yeah. That's what I'm talkin' about." She closed her eyes and grabbed the bottom hem of her shirt, fanning it back and forth, hoping to dry the sweat streaks. She lowered the visor and opened the vanity mirror to reveal a sheen of sweat covering her face and neck, hair that had gone from straight to wavy, and wispy hairs stuck to the sweat on her forehead. She snapped it closed and shoved the visor up. "I wish I hadn't looked."

Micah chuckled.

She glanced over at him and smiled. "My air conditioner doesn't work."

He angled his head toward her car. "Among other things."

"I'm trying to keep it running as long as I can."

"I'd say it's on its last leg."

"I don't want a car payment right now."

"I get that," he replied.

"Says the guy driving a Lexus."

He raised an eyebrow at her. "It's Keely's dad's car."

"Oh." She'd never pictured him as someone who would drive a fancy car like this, and hearing it wasn't his actually made her happy. Like her, he hadn't come from money. Their families had worked hard for everything they got. And she didn't like the thought that they might not have that in common anymore. Not that she would resent him if he drove a Lexus. Because if he did, it meant he had worked his butt off to get it. A strong work ethic had always been one of his most attractive qualities.

"So, you're doing it," he said. "You're living the dream."

Countless nights had been spent lying in his arms in the back of his pickup, staring up at the stars, talking about her love of photography and how she someday wanted to run her own business.

"I guess I am," she replied.

"No guessing about it. You made it happen."

She smiled over at him and found him smiling back.

"I'm so proud of you."

Her throat tightened with emotion, and she quickly turned to look out the window so he wouldn't see any runaway tears. Those words affected her more than anything had in a long time. His pride in her had always been evident when they were together. He believed in her, and had encouraged her to shoot for the stars, to dream big, because anything was possible.

Receiving that support from him again after all these years broke her heart open and spilled out feelings hidden away long ago. Those feelings were quickly followed by nudges of doubt and worry and regret—her biggest being the night she let Micah go.

Silence invaded the car. She hadn't even realized she was stuck inside her head, sinking into the memories, until she felt the weight of his hand on hers.

"Hey, where are you right now?"

Her eyes met his, and it all fell away. "Nowhere."

His expression said he didn't believe her. Not at all.

"How are *you*?" she asked, anxious to outrun thoughts of the past and focus on the present. "What do you do now?"

"I'm still in Virginia. I work for NASA. Computer engineering."

Shannon gasped. "NASA? Wow! So a Lexus probably isn't out of the question for you, huh?"

He laughed. "I don't know about that, but I do all right."

"You said you introduced Keely and Chase."

He nodded. "Chase and I went to Liberty together. I brought him and a couple friends home with me one weekend and took them to church. Keely was there, and he was awestruck."

"*Aww*, that's sweet."

"They've been together ever since."

"I knew they'd been together for a long time, but I didn't realize it had been that long." She and Keely were old high school friends, but they hadn't remained close after graduation and had only recently reconnected when Keely hired her as their wedding photographer.

"Yeah, almost eight years." He became quiet and fiddled with the air conditioner vent. "I thought we might see you at church that day."

"Uh … I don't really go there anymore." This topic always made her uneasy.

"Did you switch churches?"

"It's a long story." She wanted nothing more than to change the subject. "Gosh, I don't think I could wait eight years to get married."

"Why not?"

She gave him a look. "I mean, that's a long time to go without being together, if you know what I mean."

His eyebrows raised. "Oh, I know what you mean."

"Unless they didn't wait," she continued. "In that case, I guess it really wouldn't matter when they got married, because they're already enjoying the benefits."

His eyes widened, and his mouth dropped open a little. "Shannon McGregor, you shock me. What would your mother say if she heard you talking like this?"

"She would agree with me."

He laughed lightly. "You're right. She would."

Her strong, opinionated Italian mother had never been afraid to speak her mind. Shannon was very much like her in that way.

"I mean ... could *you* wait eight years?" Her eyes locked with his, a blush creeping over her cheeks, and she wished she could rewind time and convince her brain to go down a different path. Why had she taken this conversation straight to the gutter?

"If she was *the one*, I would wait as long as I had to." His reply came out hushed, and the look in his eyes—a look he had given her hundreds of times during the year they spent together—made her stomach flutter.

The tow truck pulled up then, breaking the spell. *Thank God.*

After ten years apart, all it took was minutes for her feelings to rush back full force. Mere minutes to undo the years she had spent trying to bury the memories. Because now that he was right in front of her—clearly settled, happy, and in a good place in his life—she couldn't help but wonder what might've been. What might have happened if she'd gone to Virginia with him like he'd asked.

Chapter 2

"Y ou made it!" Keely clasped her hands together, her face beaming with joy. She raced to Shannon and hugged her. "We waited for you."

Shannon's face heated. "No, you did not." Horrified, she looked around at the family and friends, mingling and chatting, tables containing nothing but coffee and water. Despite her worry over ruining the event, nobody seemed the least bit upset that there'd been a delay, except maybe the older woman standing next to Chase, wearing a scowl.

Keely patted Micah on the back. "Thanks, Micah."

"Not a problem. I'm going to say hello to Chase's parents." His eyes flicked to Shannon's before he walked away to Chase's side.

"Is that Chase's mom?" Shannon asked of the lady with the scowl, who reminded her of Meryl Streep's character in *The Devil Wears Prada.*

"Yeah, and ..." Keely scanned the room then pointed to a distinguished gentleman with wavy grey hair, standing next to her parents. "That's his dad."

Shannon's gaze returned to Chase and his mom, who were now chatting with Micah. "You never mentioned Micah was the best man."

Realization suddenly crossed Keely's face, and she touched her mouth with her hand. "Oh my gosh, I totally forgot you guys dated in high school. I'm so sorry."

"It was a long time ago. I was just surprised to see him, that's all." Shannon watched him, standing next to Chase, laughing. Micah peered over his shoulder in her direction, and she quickly looked at Keely, whose eyes were shifting back and forth between her and Micah.

Keely's eyes suddenly lit up and a slow smile spread. "Oh my."

"What?" Shannon asked.

"You two still have the hots for each other."

A snort escaped Shannon. "Oh, right. Ten years later."

Keely was interrupted then by the caterer with a question about serving the food. "I'm sorry, Shannon. I have to take care of this. But we *will* continue this conversation." She tucked a loose blonde curl behind her ear and pointed at Shannon. "Later."

Shannon moved to a nearby table, removed two Canon 5D MK II cameras from her bag, and attached a telephoto lens to one and a fixed width lens to the other. With one camera around her neck and the other over her shoulder—allowing her to switch quickly depending on the situation—she was ready to go.

The location was lovely. A large banquet room set high on the property of the John Ball Zoo. Floor-to-ceiling windows on three sides gave a sweeping view of the surrounding treetops and a glimpse of downtown Grand Rapids, not to mention killer natural light.

The room was abuzz with conversation. She fixed her lens on Micah and Chase talking and snapped a few shots as they laughed. She loved capturing the candid, unplanned moments, and the raw, real relationships between people. Those pictures told more of a story than any posed photo ever could.

She moved about the room, getting more shots of the guests— an elderly woman holding hands with a little girl, a small group of women laughing hysterically, some older men seriously discussing their golf games, or politics, or both.

As she circled back around the room, Keely sauntered up to Chase, whose eyes lit up at his lovely fiancée. She captured the loving way they gazed at each other and the second they came together for a tender kiss.

The sweet moment tugged at her heart. If they had been together for eight years and still looked at each other that way, then they were sure to last. Would she ever have that with someone? She glanced in Micah's direction. Maybe she'd had her chance and blown it.

Keely's sister, Becca, the matron of honor, moved about the room then, corralling everyone to the tables. With her sleek blonde tresses and petite frame, she looked more like Keely's twin than her older sister.

Once everyone was seated, Chase stood and laid his hand on Keely's shoulder.

"On behalf of myself and my beautiful bride ..." He smiled down at her. "We want to thank you all for coming to this little 'welcome to town' brunch. Some of you have traveled a great distance, and we appreciate you being with us for the next few days leading up to the wedding. This has been a long time coming—"

"Amen!" Keely's father piped in.

Laughter filled the room.

"Thanks for that, Bob." Chase cleared his throat and adjusted his tie. "We're very excited to start our married life together and to have you here with us to celebrate."

Someone tapped their water glass with a fork, which started the clinking of glasses throughout the room.

"Save it for the wedding," Chase cried.

Keely stood and slid her arms around his neck. "Speak for yourself." And she planted one on him.

Shannon grinned as she pressed the shutter release, knowing she had captured one of the cutest moments of the day.

Keely came up for air long enough to tell everyone to enjoy brunch, before she went back to kissing Chase again.

Shannon captured more of the guests' reactions, turning the camera on Keely's parents, who were all smiles, then to Chase's parents. His dad's grin was wide, but his mom wore no expression at all. She sat completely straight-faced, her eyes devoid of emotion. Shannon wondered if something was wrong with her—maybe an illness—or if she was just that unpleasant.

The group settled to a light chatter as they feasted on french toast, waffles, and home fries and sipped on mimosas, coffee, and tea. Shannon continued to move about the room, photographing the flowers on the tables, the food, the drinks, the servers. She captured everything she could.

A hand on her upper back startled her.

"Come sit with us." Keely gently nudged her.

"Oh, that's okay. You don't have to feed me. Especially after I put you so behind schedule."

"Nonsense." Keely took her arm and led her to the main table, where she retrieved an extra chair and made Micah move his chair over, so she could squeeze it in next to her own.

Real subtle, Keely.

Shannon took a seat and set her equipment on the floor by her feet, keeping one of her cameras in her lap in case she needed to capture something quickly. Her senses were immediately assaulted by Micah's cologne again. It was so unfair that he still smelled—and looked—so good after all these years. Couldn't he have just gained weight and let himself go, even a little bit? But then, part of her knew that even if he had, she would still feel something for him.

Keely passed the french toast her way while Chase motioned for a server. Next thing she knew, a plate piled high with toast and a hearty helping of home fries was set in front of her. Micah placed the syrup bottle on the table by her plate. She swallowed hard. None of this was good for her. It was definitely not on her list of approved foods. But she felt embarrassed to say so.

She lifted her glass of water to Keely to avoid taking a bite of all the sugar in front of her. "To the future Mr. and Mrs. Pennington."

Everyone at their table lifted a glass and toasted to the couple.

Shannon was thankful to be included at the main table, but she hoped nobody would notice if she didn't eat much of the heap of food before her.

Her brother, Duncan, often told her it was okay to splurge every once in a while, but there were reasons for her diet. He knew there were. Reasons she seldom shared with anyone unless she absolutely had to.

She took a tiny bite of the syrup-soaked toast and sighed. *So good.* She couldn't remember the last time she'd had sugar, actually. Most days, she started with a glass of almond milk and a spinach and cheese omelet. And she couldn't help but feel as if each sugary bite she took was harming her and undoing the habits she had worked so hard to attain.

"How's your family?" Micah asked as everyone fell into conversation again.

"They're good."

"Your parents?"

"Doing well. Keeping busy. Mama wants to travel more. She's set on going back to Italy to visit the family soon. It's been five years since they were there last."

"I bet she misses them."

"She does. Very much."

"How's your sister?" Micah took a bite of his french toast and a little syrup dribbled over his chin.

Shannon fought the urge to reach out and wipe it away. "Sophia lives in New York and works in fashion now."

"I heard that."

It didn't surprise her that he had heard news about her family. They had plenty of mutual friends from high school and church.

"How long has she been living there?" he asked.

Shannon thought for a few seconds. "It's been almost nine years. She went right after she graduated, even though our parents freaked out about her being in the city after 9/11. It had only been a year, and they didn't want her there, but Sophia was determined. She loves it, and she's starting to make a name for herself."

Micah smiled. "That's awesome. I remember her always wearing the craziest outfits. She definitely had her own sense of style."

"That's an understatement." Sophia was bold, unique, and confident in personality and fashion sense. And she was doing exactly what she was meant to do—dress women in beautiful clothing that make them feel good about themselves.

"What's Duncan up to?" Micah lifted his coffee cup and took a sip.

Shannon tried not to watch the cup touch his lips, but failed.

He noticed and gave her the tiniest hint of a smile as he set the cup on the saucer with a clink.

She blushed. "Duncan's doing great. Traveling a lot. He does freelance graphic design, which he can pretty much do anywhere.

He's probably gone more than he's home. I think he's still searching for his place in the world."

"Is he traveling right now?" he asked.

"He's been out west in Denver for a couple months—some kind of design job for an outdoor gear company, I think. He's been hiking up mountains in his free time. He says it's beautiful there. But he comes home tomorrow night, and I can't wait."

"You two are still close?"

She nodded.

"I always loved how close you were with your family."

"I know." Her heart tugged at his comment, knowing he'd never had the opportunity to know his parents, and had been raised by an aunt he didn't really get along with.

"How's Granny McG?" he asked.

A laugh escaped her at the nickname only Micah had ever called her grandmother. "Oh my gosh, I forgot about that."

Micah laughed along with her, and she didn't miss the way his eyes traveled over her face, like he was taking it all in.

"Uh ... she's good. Still going strong at ninety-six. Still baking the most delicious desserts and trying to fatten us all up." *Not that I eat them anymore.*

"I seriously had to buy bigger jeans after the way she fed us that Christmas." He winked at her.

That Christmas was probably her favorite of any Christmas ever. There had been something so magical about being with him and having him there with her family.

Her thoughts turned somber. "We lost Papi about five years ago."

"I heard. I'm so sorry. I thought about coming back for the funeral, but I couldn't get away."

She waved it off. "Oh, that's fine. Thanks for thinking of us, though."

He gave her a sweet, sympathetic smile.

"You should stop by and say hello to Nana," Shannon told him. "She would love to see you."

He shifted his eyes away from hers. "Maybe."

Too much, Shannon. She wished she could keep her mouth shut sometimes. It was true, Nana would love to see him after all these years. But then, she hadn't really explained to her grandmother what happened with her and Micah, and she would rather not rehash the past, so maybe it wasn't a good idea after all.

"Hey, did your dad ever find any of his family in Scotland? I remember he was on a search for them."

She nodded. "A few cousins. I know Dad would love to get to Scotland one of these days to meet them. Especially now that Papi's gone."

Micah's phone suddenly buzzed on the table.

Shannon couldn't help but notice the name on the screen— Autumn.

He glanced over at her, quickly snatching the phone as he stood and answered. "Hey." He wandered across the room to talk.

Autumn must be his fiancée. Or soon-to-be fiancée. Her heart sank at the thought, but it served her right after the way she had left things between them. Seeing him again after all these years and knowing he would never be hers was an excruciating torture that she deserved. Even worse would be seeing the two of them together. But she would have to get over it. Autumn would most certainly be joining him for the wedding, and Shannon wondered how soon she would be arriving. Was she pretty? Did she make him happy? Her mind spun out of control. What if they wanted a picture taken together? How humiliating that would be to photograph her ex with his girlfriend. She imagined lifting the camera, peering through the viewfinder, seeing the two of them gazing into each other's eyes with complete and utter love. A wave of nausea moved through her body. She took a drink of water, praying the little bit of food she'd eaten wouldn't come back up.

When Micah returned to the table, she smiled politely, still pushing down the queasiness in her stomach.

"Sorry. Work call."

Was that the truth? Had she jumped to conclusions? Was Autumn really a work colleague? The only way she would know for sure was to ask. "Uh, who's—"

The clinking of glasses interrupted her question, and she turned to see the happy couple kissing again. She yanked her camera from her lap and fired off a few shots of them at close range. She checked the image on the back of her camera.

"Nice." Micah had leaned forward to see the photo and was so close his breath tickled her neck.

She swallowed hard as she turned her head to look at him, and he backed slowly away. "It helps that they're a good-looking couple."

"There's always that," Micah replied with a smile.

"*Awww*, thanks, Shannon." Keely had obviously overheard them.

She and Chase moved to the other tables to mingle with their guests, and Shannon scooted her chair out and looked at Micah. "I should really get back to work."

"Oh, sure." He motioned toward her camera. "Don't let me keep you."

She stood and gathered her equipment, then pushed the chair back in. "It was nice catching up a little."

"Yeah, it was."

It took extreme focus to make her feet move away from the table—away from him—but she lifted her camera and snapped a few pictures of Chase and Keely chatting with guests and got back in the groove of photographing the remainder of the event.

When the meal concluded and the event began to wrap up, Shannon hung around until mostly bridal party members and immediate family remained.

"So, we'll see you tomorrow afternoon for the bridal shower, right?" Keely asked as she gave Shannon a tight hug.

Shannon nodded as Keely let her go. "Two o'clock. And I have the directions."

"Perfect. Do you need a ride home?"

Shannon shook her head. "Oh, it's okay. I can find someone to drive me."

"Micah!"

Shannon startled at Keely's loud cry. "Keely, it's fine."

But there was no stopping her as she waved Micah over. "Shannon needs a ride home," Keely announced as Micah strode toward them.

His eyes lit up. "No problem. I'll take you wherever you need to go," he told her.

Nerves took over. She probably could've called Jamie, but now that Micah was standing there with that sweet look on his face, offering her a ride, she would be crazy to pass up the chance to spend more time with him. She had questions she was dying to ask, but would twenty minutes in the car be enough time to get the answers she wanted?

Chapter 3

The entire car smelled like vanilla. Was it her shampoo? Her body lotion? Some kind of perfume? Or did she naturally smell that good? All Micah was sure of was that from the moment his eyes connected with hers next to her broken down car, his heart had been beating at a slightly faster rate than normal. Ten years wasn't enough to erase the way he had always felt when she was near. The longing for her was still there, but so was the pain.

"Do you still play baseball?" she asked as he drove toward her apartment.

He nodded. "I play on a league at work. It's still the best game there ever was."

"Sure it is." She laughed, and it filled his heart with joy.

How had he survived so long without hearing that sound?

"Sorry, you know how I feel about baseball."

He chuckled. Shannon wasn't a fan of the sport. She found it tedious. But despite that, she had gone to every game his senior year and cheered him on—well, almost every game. The one game she'd missed, he had performed miserably, which had him believing she was his good luck charm. But once he got to college, he realized that had been a silly teenage fantasy. Liberty had one of the best baseball teams in the Big South Conference, and he hadn't needed Shannon there to do well. Even so, he'd missed having her in the stands, rooting for the team, hugging him after the game, whispering how proud she was of him.

"Do you miss it?"

He looked over at her questioningly, his mind stuck on her congratulatory hugs.

"Playing college ball?" she asked.

Of course he did. It had been his life for four years at Liberty. He had made some of his best friends on that team—Chase included—and sometimes he longed to go back there and relive those glory days all over again.

"I do. It was a happy time in my life."

"And you're not happy now?"

"I'm happy." *Sort of.*

"Good." Her smooth, lovely lips curved up on both sides revealing perfectly straight teeth on top and bottom. He was taken aback. "Did you get braces?"

"Mhmm. Years ago." She smiled purposely to show off the results.

Her smile was even more gorgeous than before, but part of him had always liked the way her bottom teeth angled a little to one side and weren't perfectly straight across the front. "Looks good."

"I hated my crooked smile."

"I thought it was adorable. But most of the time I was looking at your lips, not your teeth." The words slipped out before he could stop them. *Did I just say that out loud?*

Her cheeks were suddenly the softest shade of pink, and he knew if he reached out and touched them, he would find warmth there. But he didn't move. He didn't touch. He kept his hands to himself. He had to, whether he wanted to or not.

The car grew quiet for a few minutes. He was sure his comment had made her uncomfortable.

"Who's Autumn?" Shannon broke the silence.

"How do you know about Autumn?"

She avoided eye contact. "Oh, I saw her name on your phone. You said it was work."

He glanced over and saw her eyeing him.

"Was it? Or is she ..."

Was Shannon jealous? She sure seemed to be. "Is she what?" He wanted to hear her say it.

"Your girlfriend?" She stared straight ahead. "Fiancée?" She began chewing on her bottom lip like she always had when she was nervous. "Wife?"

As if on reflex, he reached out and took her chin between his thumb and forefinger. Her eyes grew wide, but she obviously remembered what it meant when he used to do that, because she released her lip from her teeth as he let go. Touching her had been a mistake. Now that he'd done it once, he wanted to do it again.

Her eyelashes batted against her cheeks as she stared at him, awaiting an answer.

"We probably shouldn't get too personal this weekend." The attraction he still felt for her was making him say and do stupid things.

"Oh. It's just ... I heard you were planning to propose to someone."

He didn't answer at first. He couldn't. He felt the sudden need to undo a button or two at the collar of his dress shirt. The girl she referred to wasn't Autumn, it was Jacqueline, his college sweetheart. She was the one he had been dating since senior year, the one he adored—at first. She was the one for whom he had bought the largest diamond he could afford.

But even after five years spent with Jacqueline, he couldn't go through with it. Sure, they had a good relationship and decent chemistry, but something had been missing. Not once had she walked into a room and elicited the kind of response he got when Shannon was near—dry mouth, heart pounding in his ears, blood surging. He had loved her, just not enough. He wished it hadn't taken him so long to figure that out. And the fact that he was still skittish about commitment because of Shannon ticked him off.

"Autumn's my girlfriend, yeah." That wasn't the whole truth, and he didn't elaborate to tell her it wasn't serious with Autumn, because he wanted her to think it was. He wanted her jealous, hurt, and regretful over breaking up with him.

"Oh."

"She'll be here on Friday for the rehearsal," he blurted, hoping to get more of a reaction.

"Well, I look forward to meeting her." She responded politely, but he knew that forlorn look in her eyes and the way her bottom lip stuck out in a little pout. She wasn't happy that he had a girlfriend or that she was coming to town. And that fact pleased him more than it should have.

"Take the next left to my apartment."

I shouldn't care about her at all after what she did to me.

"All the way to the end. Building three."

And I definitely shouldn't go anywhere near her apartment.

He turned his car into an empty parking spot in front of her building. "Can I walk you to your door?"

Oy! Why can't I just leave well enough alone?

"No." Shannon shook her head.

"Carry your bag for you?" *What is the matter with me?*

"Not necessary." Her answers were clipped.

"Use your bathroom?"

Her disapproval was obvious in the way her mouth tilted to one side.

"What? I gotta go." He really did.

She sighed. "All right. I guess. But only for a minute."

Micah opened the door and retrieved her camera bag before she had a chance to change her mind.

Shannon let them in the building, and they climbed the two flights of stairs to Apartment C.

Vanilla again. Everywhere vanilla. He could get lost in it. Just close his eyes and inhale it all until he was high on that scent. And better yet if Shannon were wrapped up in his arms where he could enjoy the fragrance up close and personal. *Oh, I'm in trouble here.*

She stepped to the side to let him into the apartment, then closed the door behind them.

The sound of the door clicking shut made his pulse stutter for some reason. Maybe the fact that they were alone together in her apartment, alone for the first time in ten years. And that he couldn't seem to control his thoughts when it came to her.

"So, this is it." She waved her arms back and forth as she pointed out the kitchen, the dining area, a bathroom, and her bedroom.

Her bedroom door was open, and he could see her bed was made with a simple white comforter and a few throw pillows, and folded on the end of her bed was her favorite patchwork quilt—the one her grandmother and great aunts had made for her as a high school graduation gift.

Something inside him stirred, remembering lying in the back of his truck with her, snuggled up under that very quilt. The sky had been so dark that night, the stars so bright. There had been a chill in the air, but he hadn't felt it. She'd been so warm, so soft. Nothing and nobody on the planet had existed but the two of them. That was the last time he'd ever held her in his arms, felt her body against his, tasted her sweet kisses.

"Micah?" Her voice broke through his thoughts.

"Huh?"

"I thought you had to use the bathroom."

"Right." His pulse was racing. "I was just checking out the apartment."

"And?"

"It's an apartment."

She frowned. "Well, it's all my budget will allow."

"I wasn't dissing it, but it's not the house on the water you always dreamed of."

The frown became a scowl. "I haven't stopped dreaming, Micah. I'm working hard to get where I want to be."

"I believe it." He wasn't sure how this conversation had gone south so quickly. Maybe the earlier girlfriend conversation. He wanted to turn things around. And fast. "I believe in you. I always have."

Her expression softened.

"If there's anyone who can dream big, then set goals to get there, it's you. I've always admired that about you." *And so many other things.*

There it was. The smile that could make a man weak in the knees.

"Thank you." There was a shyness in her he wasn't used to seeing.

His fingers twitched at the sight of a section of her hair that had fallen from her ponytail and slipped forward over her left eye, covering her slightly downturned face like a veil. He squeezed them into a fist, fighting himself, wanting badly to run them through the softness, to tuck the silky strands behind that cute little ear of hers.

21

"Well, thanks for the ride." She was fidgeting.

"Do you want me to go?" he asked.

She tilted her head up, her hair sliding away from her face again, and her rich brown eyes met his. "I'm sure you have better things to do. Wedding stuff with Chase or something."

He shrugged his shoulders. He did. The guys were all getting together at Keely's parents' house to grill out, but that wasn't for hours.

"It's fine. You can go, Micah."

"Do you have plans tonight?" He had no control over the words coming from his mouth.

"Big plans," she replied.

"Oh, okay."

"Yep, just me and my computer and a few memory cards worth of pictures from brunch."

When he looked at her again, her lips were curved up and her eyes twinkled mischievously.

He wanted to hate her, to yell at her, to tell her how much she had hurt him, but when she looked at him like that, all he could do was grin. He was completely powerless against her.

"What did you have in mind?" she asked.

His mind was blank. There was no plan. He hadn't meant to ask her.

"Dinner?" His eyebrows raised a little in question.

She nodded once. "Dinner." A slow smile spread across her face. "And I've got another idea."

He couldn't help but grin. She'd always been the best at spontaneity. Some of their best times together had been when they'd run off somewhere together for a day. No set plans. Just the two of them driving around in his truck, stopping who knows where.

"Should I be worried? I mean, we're not gonna end up in the U.P., are we?"

She shrugged her shoulders. "I love the U.P."

"I know you do, that's why I asked."

He had thought if he ever saw Shannon again, he'd feel nothing but hurt and betrayal and anger toward her. Those feelings were definitely still there. It would take more than seeing her for a day for him to forgive and forget. But that gravitational pull was still there too. The force that had always kept him orbiting around her—the brightest light in the center of his universe. Until she wasn't. His heart clenched a little thinking of how dim his life had been for the past ten years without her.

Despite the hurt he still felt, there was also a strong desire to get to know her as she was now, to learn how the past decade had changed her. And maybe that would lead him to the truth about their sudden, unexpected breakup.

He'd have to bow out of the cookout, but Chase would understand.

"Do you mind if I change first and pack a bag with some bear spray?" she teased.

His eyes followed her as she moved into her bedroom, and his mouth went dry when she glanced back over her shoulder and slowly closed the door between them.

He closed his eyes and ran his fingers through his hair as he inhaled deeply and slowly let it out. How in the world was he going to get through an afternoon of sitting next to her? Her and that darn vanilla?

To distract himself, he wandered around her living room, looking at the books on her shelves—photography books, photography magazines, photography manuals. Seeing her do her thing at brunch had filled him with so much pride. She had started her business like she'd wanted, and she was darn good at it. He'd seen her website. He knew her work, and he knew it well. But he'd never admit that to her. He'd never tell her how he had stalked her online over the years or about the multiple emails he had drafted to her but never sent.

Framed photos were arranged on the top of her book shelf— Shannon with her family, with friends, with other guys. He wondered if one of them was her boyfriend, and his chest tightened at the thought. If she'd met someone, he couldn't fault her for it. Ten years was a long time, and he wanted her to be happy. He'd just always assumed her happiness would include him.

The door squeaked when it opened, and Shannon stepped into the living room wearing a simple white v-neck t-shirt with a pair of khaki capri pants that hugged her curves just right.

He thought his mouth had been dry before, but now it was as arid as the Sahara.

She gave him a cute little smile as she walked to the shoe rack by the door and bent down to put on some strappy brown sandals. Her long, wavy hair fell all around her in a cascade of black silk with milk chocolate highlights.

His eyes fixed on her ankle as she worked on the buckle, and he had to turn his gaze to the ceiling to keep from following the curve of her leg all the way up to her backside.

He escaped to the kitchen and opened her refrigerator in search of water. It surprised him to find it filled to the brim with greens—lettuces, kale, broccoli, green beans, zucchini, cucumbers, celery, even green apples. There were the usual staples as well—milk, eggs, cheese, butter—but so much green.

Shannon cleared her throat. "Make yourself at home."

"On a bit of a health kick?" he asked as he peeked around the door at her.

"Did you need something?" She raised an eyebrow at him as she stepped closer.

"Water." He was burning up from her nearness, despite the fact that he was standing in front of the open refrigerator.

She walked to the cupboard, retrieved a glass, and filled it from the tap. "Water." She held it out to him with a smug look on her face. "It comes from a thing called a faucet," she teased.

He tilted his head and smirked, pushing the fridge door closed. He took the glass from her, avoiding her fingers in the exchange. Over the rim, he watched her as he drank. Her eyes were fixed on his, which made him self-conscious.

Her beauty overwhelmed him. Even more so than it used to. It felt like junior year of high school all over again. Her looks had intimidated him at first, but her warmth, kindness, and easygoing personality had quickly assuaged his nerves, and he'd never been anything but comfortable with her after that.

There was something different about her now—a standoffishness he hadn't known in her before. Maybe it was because they hadn't seen each other in ten years. Maybe it was the fact that he had a girlfriend. Or maybe she felt awkward about how they'd left things back then. How she'd left things, actually.

He set the glass on the counter and looked at the fridge again. "Seriously, that's a lot of green in there."

"I try to eat healthy, that's all. I don't cook big meals or anything, so ..." She drifted off to somewhere far away for a few moments.

Micah wished he could invade her thoughts, know where she was, but it obviously wasn't a place she wanted to share with him, so he motioned his head toward the bathroom. "Guess I should use the bathroom. That's why we came up here, after all."

"Right."

He stepped into the little room, taking in the sea-foam colored towels and washcloths hanging over the bar and a vanilla candle on the counter by the sink. He looked at himself in the mirror and reached up to open the cabinet there, pushing aside what he knew her reaction would be—especially after snooping in her refrigerator. Lotion, nail polish, hair products—all the usual girly stuff. His eyes suddenly latched on to a round pink case on the bottom shelf. He took it in his hand before he could stop himself and popped the lid, already knowing what it was before he even saw the label inside. *Why is Shannon on birth control?*

His first reaction was to question her on it. Was one of those guys in the pictures her boyfriend? Was she sleeping with him? It was none of his business, really. But then why did he want to pummel somebody right now? He put it back and closed the cabinet, so flustered that he left the bathroom without using it.

"Let's go."

Once in the car, Shannon directed him to drive from her Kentwood apartment toward East Grand Rapids. He drove in silence, doing nothing to hide his agitation, while she pointed out buildings and houses that had been renovated or demolished. If she noticed the tension in his shoulders or how tightly he gripped the steering wheel, she ignored it.

Shannon pointed at a house they were passing. "Do you remember C.J. Doyle? He still lives there with his parents. Fired from yet another job, I heard."

She mentioned a few more places along their route, but he couldn't concentrate on what she was saying. That pink case in her bathroom was blocking out everything else.

"How often do you get back to Michigan?" she asked.

"I've been back a few times, but not for years." Had she really not known that? Up until that moment, he thought maybe she'd wondered about him over the years—perhaps missed him—but now he doubted if she'd thought about him at all.

"I thought we could drive around and see how much this place has changed since you left."

Micah drove up and down familiar streets from their high school days, and Shannon served as tour guide, sharing about local restaurants and businesses that had come and gone.

"Is something wrong?" she asked as they drove into Gaslight Village.

"Nothing."

He wasn't sure if she believed him or not, but she turned her attention back to the street.

"That building right there is where Jamie and I will soon have our own studio space."

He looked at the old brick building with Simon Walker Photographer displayed in the window. "Very nice. Great location."

"I know. We're so excited. Simon relocated to Hastings to open a studio with his new wife, Maggie. They're photographer friends of ours."

"So, he's giving you the space?"

"We're meeting with the owner of the building this week to talk about taking over the space."

"That's exciting."

"I know." Her smile was the biggest he'd seen on her all day.

Micah drove past their old high school, and Shannon quieted with her hands clasped in her lap. She said nothing about the school. Despite their friendly conversation, he could tell she was holding back with him. Things were different now. They'd changed. They'd grown up, apart from each other. They were different people now. Weren't they?

Being around her felt the same to him. But she was obviously different if she was sleeping with someone. He never thought she'd compromise her morals like that. Her purity was something she had held tightly to, something she planned to save for her future husband. Thinking she might not have waited brought on a myriad of emotions—jealousy, anger, insecurity, to name a few—and he wanted to say something, to confront her on it. But the words that kept trudging through his mind weren't angry or confrontational, they were heavy with disappointment.

I wish she'd saved herself for me.

"Do you want to go see my grandma?" she asked out of nowhere.

His mouth fell open a little. It was more personal than he'd expected her to get. Her grandma was one of the most important people in her life, and when she had mentioned it at brunch, he thought she was simply being polite. "Are you sure that wouldn't be too awkward?"

"I just ... I thought you might want to see her. Me and my brilliant ideas."

He stopped at the light at the end of Wealthy Street. The crisp blue water of Reeds Lake was before them. Oh, man, he wished he'd used her bathroom.

Shannon fidgeted. "I'm sorry I suggested it."

He moved his hand to rest atop hers without really thinking. The innate need to calm and assure her was strong. "I'd love to see her."

Her lips pressed together and curved up in a little smile. "Good. She'll be so happy to see you."

"Ya think?"

"Of course, Micah. She loved you. Even more than me, I think."

He laughed for the first time since they got into the car. "I doubt that."

"You'd be surprised."

He turned right onto Lakeside Drive and put his blinker on to go right at the next street.

"Go straight here," Shannon instructed.

"Straight? Did your grandma move?"

"Yeah," she replied.

He drove straight for a couple miles.

"Turn left at the next light, then right on Woodcliff."

This route was so familiar, he could've driven it blindfolded. "Why didn't you just tell me we were going to your parents' house?"

Shannon shrugged. "I thought you might not want to go."

"Your grandma lives there now?"

"She moved in shortly after we lost Papi."

The McGregor home was nestled on a quiet residential street. A thousand memories surfaced as he pulled into their driveway. He looked up at the window that had once been Shannon's and remembered climbing the trellis to get to her. She had cracked her window three inches and refused to open it fully until he declared his love for her to the entire neighborhood. Not only that ... his declaration had to be done in song—her favorite song at the time, "I Don't Want To Miss A Thing" by Aerosmith. And he had done it. Out of tune and all. Unashamedly and with plenty of gusto. And when she'd opened that window and pressed her soft lips against his, it had been totally worth it.

Shannon cleared her throat, grabbing his attention.

"We're here." She opened the door and got out of the car.

He cut the engine and followed.

She floated past him humming that very song. Of course she knew that's what he'd been thinking about. It had been the source of her continuous teasing and their inside joke for months after. The bright afternoon sun glinted off her eyes as she glanced back over her shoulder at him, and his heart skipped a beat.

Were things really so different now?

As he walked toward the door, his nerves kicked up a notch at the thought of stepping foot in this house again. He had told her they shouldn't get too personal this weekend, but here he was, walking straight into the past.

It was so easy and familiar being with her, though. He wanted to know everything about her life, all she'd been through since he left.

He wanted to tell her everything—about Jacqueline, Autumn, his life in Virginia—but would she even care to hear it?

One thing he knew for sure, he needed to be careful about getting too close to her. His heart needed to stay guarded, because she could break it again. So easily. And he didn't know if he could survive that again.

Chapter 4

"ana?" Shannon called out as they walked through to the sun room at the back of the house. It was Nana's favorite place to spend her days. She'd sit and read for hours, happily lost in the pages of books, sipping on her tea, watching the birds at the feeders in the backyard.

Shannon stepped through the door, but Nana wasn't there. She turned abruptly, and Micah ran right into her. Her hands gripped the fabric of his dress shirt to keep from falling backwards.

"Sorry," they both blurted simultaneously.

"My fault." She wished she could stop herself from blushing. He probably thought she had the flu or a fever after all the blushing she'd done so far that day.

"Samantha?" Nana called out from the kitchen. "Is that you?"

"It's Shannon, Nana." She led Micah through the house to where her grandmother, Irene McGregor, stood in the kitchen.

"I thought you were your mother." Nana didn't look up from her place at the counter. Her wrinkled, crooked fingers slowly pressed dough into a pie pan. "She said she'd be right back."

"Nana, I brought you a visitor."

Nana's eyes finally lifted from the pan to Shannon's face and then past her to Micah.

"Hey, Granny McG." He gave her a little wave.

Her mouth dropped open, and she lifted her hands in the air. "Oh my heavens! Is that really you? Is that my Micah?" She brushed her floury hands against her apron and shuffled across the floor.

Micah stepped around Shannon and closed the distance, wrapping his arms gently around Nana as she clung to him and laid her head on his chest.

"Oh, dear boy, you have been missed." Nana held on to him tightly.

Shannon's heart squeezed as Nana used the edge of her apron to wipe tears from her eyes.

"I've missed you, too, Granny." He glanced back at Shannon.

"Told you," Shannon mouthed.

"Come sit down and have a piece of pie," Nana insisted, moving to the cupboard to get him a plate, then cutting a slice of another pie that sat cooling on the counter.

"I'm gonna go wash my hands." Micah bolted for the hallway bathroom.

"There's a sink right here, dear," Nana called after him.

"He had a big glass of water earlier." Shannon said with a laugh.

Nana chuckled.

Shannon motioned toward the end of the counter, noticing three more pies on the far end. "What are all these pies for, Nana?"

"Church bake sale," she replied.

Shannon was in awe of her grandmother for being heartily involved in church at her age, giving of herself for others, still spreading Jesus' love to everyone she met. Nana was an inspiration to her and always had been.

But her own relationship with God wasn't like Nana's. Not anymore. Not since He allowed her dreams to shatter.

Micah returned and took a seat at the kitchen table, and Nana set a plate of pie in front of him. "Do you like strawberry rhubarb?"

He had a large bite of the pie in his mouth before she even finished her question. "*Mmm.*"

Nana smiled proudly, then shifted her eyes to Shannon's. She didn't say anything, only gave her a little smile in return. Shannon knew her grandmother. That look said more than words ever could. She was happy Micah was there. She had loved the two of them together.

"Don't you want some?" Micah asked Shannon. "I know you're on a health kick, but you do treat yourself sometimes, don't you?"

She and her grandmother exchanged a look.

"I only have one slice to spare, and it's for you," Nana told him.

"I'm not very hungry anyway." Shannon was grateful that Nana had covered for her. When she'd found Micah staring into her fridge earlier, she'd felt put on the spot. Not that it was strange for people to want to eat healthy, but she didn't want to get into the real reason she ate the way she did. Micah would be gone by Sunday, so it really wasn't worth explaining. It wouldn't make a difference anyway.

Nana went back to slowly pressing the dough, her fingers shaking a little as she worked.

"Can I help, Nana?" Shannon asked.

"Oh, these darn fingers don't work as well as they used to."

Shannon took one of her mother's aprons from near the pantry door and lifted it over her head, reaching for the strings. She had them both in hand but kept dropping one when she tried to tie them behind her back.

"Let me." Micah stood and moved behind her. He was close. So close she could feel his breath against the back of her neck. He took the strings, twisted them together, and pulled them tight. His fingers brushed against her lower back as he worked to form them into a bow, and she hoped he didn't notice her tremble at his slight touch. "Voila!" He rested his hands on her hips. "All done."

She glanced over her shoulder at him, trying to act like his proximity hadn't just warmed her all over. "Thank you."

"My pleasure." He released her and returned to his pie.

Shannon took over filling the pie plates with dough. Nana spread some flour on the counter and handed her the rolling pin to roll the dough for another while she went about adding fruit filling to the pies.

Micah set his plate in the sink and walked across the room.

Shannon's eyes followed him to the apron hook, and she cracked up when he put on her mom's frilliest floral apron. "That's a good look on you."

He did a little spin, then came to stand next to her with a playful expression on his face. He grabbed a little flour from the counter and flicked it at her.

Shannon's mouth fell open.

He ran his finger over the counter, drawing an *S* in the white powder.

She looked over at him just as his fingertip connected with the bridge of her nose, leaving behind a line of white. Her stomach fluttered, remembering the last time they had played with flour in this very kitchen and the way that had ended.

"Don't," she told him, becoming serious as she wiped the flour from her nose.

His expression turned solemn, and he took over rolling pin duty while Shannon helped Nana lay the top crust over the fruit fillings and pinch the edges of the dough together.

Once the pies were baking in the oven, they put away their aprons, Nana poured them all some iced tea, and they went to the sun porch to chat. Nana took her usual rocking chair, and Shannon sat down on the end of the two-person wicker love seat closest to Nana, thinking Micah would probably opt for the single chair on the other side of the room facing Nana. Instead, he planted himself right next to Shannon on the love seat. It wasn't very spacious, so his elbow pushed into her ribs. She shifted a bit to the right, and he lifted his arm and rested it across the back of the seat. That was way worse. They each had enough room now, but there was no space between them. His arm was along her shoulders, his side against hers, the side of his thigh pressed against hers. She crossed her leg to move it away from his, but it didn't help. He was so close. She had to fight the instinct to sink into him like she always had. It would've been so easy to fall into that again.

"What brings you back to Grand Rapids?" Nana took a sip of her tea and rocked slowly.

"A wedding."

"Oh? Anyone I know?" she asked.

"My buddy, Chase, from college is marrying a girl we went to high school with, Keely Crawford." He touched Shannon's shoulder for an instant when he said Keely's name.

"I remember that name. Wasn't she the homecoming queen?"

Shannon nodded. "That's right, Nana. You have such a good memory."

"Thank the Lord for that." A momentary shadow fell over her.

Shannon reached over and squeezed her hand. Nana's sister, Alice, had suffered for years with dementia, and it had been a fear of hers that she would have to go through the same.

"I'm so happy to see the two of you together." Nana smiled, her eyes bright among all the wrinkles. "Are you going to the wedding with him?" she asked.

"I'm actually the wedding photographer. That's how we bumped into each other again."

Confusion crossed Nana's face for a moment. "Oh, I thought maybe ..." She waved her hand in the air. "Never mind. Don't mind an old lady like me."

"You thought maybe, what?" Micah asked.

Shannon wished he had let it go.

Nana shifted in her seat a little and looked at them seriously. "I thought maybe you both finally realized what I've known for years. That you two belong together."

"Nana, please." Shannon willed her to change the subject.

Nana shrugged her shoulders. "I don't have a lot of time left on this earth, so I'm just gonna tell it like it is."

Micah chuckled at that.

Shannon's head whipped to the side, her mouth agape, eyes locked on Micah. "That's not funny."

He pressed his lips together and quieted.

"Life is short, and there are no guarantees. You never know what will happen tomorrow. Say what you need to say, and say it now. Make it right before it's too late. Take it from someone who knows."

Micah turned to face Shannon and raised his eyebrows.

Flustered, she stood and walked out of the room.

Nana's voice followed her. "Was it something I said?"

"Excuse me for a minute," Micah replied.

Shannon felt him follow her across the house to the kitchen.

"Come on, Shannon. Don't be like this," he pleaded.

"You should go back and catch up with her. I'll wait here for the pies." She stopped next to the oven.

He stopped beside her and took hold of her upper arm.

The spot he touched was as hot as if she had leaned against the heated oven door.

"I don't want to talk about ... us," she explained.

"I know I said let's not get too personal this weekend, but I think it's too late for that. Don't you?"

She shook her head. "It doesn't have to be. We can keep things polite and friendly. We don't have to rehash everything, because it's not going to change anything."

His eyes locked with hers.

She hoped he understood, because she really didn't want to dig up all those old emotions. The real reason she had ended things and the pain she carried with her every day over letting him go were too much to deal with.

His gaze dropped to her lips, and a heat spread over her face and down her neck.

"Please, go back to Nana," she whispered.

He looked into her eyes once more and swallowed hard before releasing her arm and returning to the porch.

Shannon leaned back against the counter facing the oven. If she let him, Micah would upset her entire world. But in the process, he would ruin his own happiness, and she couldn't allow him to do that.

Chapter 5

Bringing Micah home to her parents' house had been a mistake. She didn't know what she'd been thinking. She *hadn't* been thinking really. And how could she possibly go to dinner with him now? Seeing him with Nana, joking around, simply being in his presence, had stirred up so many feelings. The more time she spent with him, the more difficult it would be when he left. She needed to get out of there and bow out on dinner.

The sound of the front door opening distracted her from her thoughts.

"Shannon?" Her mother, Samantha, called from the doorway.

Shannon met her mother and relieved her of a couple grocery bags she was carrying.

"I thought you had something for Keely's wedding today."

"I did. Brunch this morning, and I have a bridal shower tomorrow."

Mama followed her into the kitchen, and the two of them went about emptying the groceries and putting them away.

"Wow! You finished a lot of pies while I was gone!" Samantha called across the house to her mother-in-law.

"We helped," Shannon told her.

"We?" Her mother looked at her questioningly.

"Hello, Mrs. McGregor." Micah entered the room then with Nana.

Surprise flickered across Mama's face. "Well, I wasn't expecting this." She moved toward Micah and embraced him. "It's been a long time, Micah. How have you been?"

"I've been well, thanks. How are you?"

"Can't complain. Are you still in Virginia?"

Micah nodded.

Shannon didn't hear anything they said after that. The three of them were chatting like no time had passed, like they could pick up where they left off, but Shannon couldn't do that. She had to keep some distance. It was already happening—the doubt, the second-guessing. She believed her decision to end their relationship was right. Her mind knew it. But when she was with him, her heart told her otherwise.

On top of her mixed-up emotions, she had to consider his girlfriend's feelings. If Micah was *her* boyfriend, she wouldn't appreciate him spending time with an ex. She didn't want to be *that* girl, causing problems between them, messing up his happiness.

"Would you like to stay for dinner?" Mama's words caught her attention.

"We can't," Shannon blurted.

Micah's eyes met hers, and she shook her head at him.

"Thank you for the invitation," Micah replied, "but we really should be going. It was great catching up with you both."

Mama and Nana both showered him with hugs and kisses. Nana sent him away with a Tupperware container filled with several pieces of pie—even though she'd told him she only had the one to spare—and he thanked her with a kiss on the cheek.

"Shannon." Mama stopped her on her way out the door and spoke quietly so only she could hear. "Are you all right?"

"I don't know." She really didn't.

Her mother hugged her tight. "Ti amo, mia bella figlia."

"Ti amo."

"Come for lunch on Sunday to welcome your brother home."

"I will." Shannon squeezed once more before letting go and catching up with Micah in the driveway.

"Thanks for suggesting this," he said as they neared his car. "It was really good to see them again."

Shannon's phone went off with a text notification from Simon asking if they'd met with the building owner yet. She'd reply later.

But right now, she needed to deal with the dilemma at hand. "I, uh …
I think I'm gonna pass on dinner."

He stopped walking and stared over at her. "Why? Get a better
offer?"

What a weird thing for him to say. "No, I just need to be rested
for the bridal shower tomorrow afternoon. And I really do need to get
all of today's pictures backed up."

He shook his head, clearly not believing her, and climbed into the
car.

Shannon got in and buckled her seatbelt, glancing over at Micah,
who had never been very good at hiding his emotions. He'd been
upset earlier. And now, he was clearly disappointed.

"Is this because of the flour?" he asked.

"What?"

"The moment with the flour earlier."

She felt his stare and avoided eye contact.

"I remembered it, too."

She looked out the window. "I don't know what you mean."

"Yes, you do."

He was right. He had always been able to see right through her.
She couldn't hide that she knew exactly what he was talking about—
that floury afternoon in the kitchen all those years ago. The day they
made sugar cookies together. Well, they tried, anyway.

*"Wait!" Shannon scolded Micah as he plopped a ball of dough
on the countertop and began flattening it with the rolling pin. She
grabbed the dough and smashed it back into a ball.*

"Hey! You ruined it," he said.

*"You have to spread some flour on the counter first or the dough
will stick." It had already started to, so she scraped it off then scooped
some flour and dumped it on the counter, spreading it around with
her hand to cover the area they would need for the dough. "See."*

*He ran his finger through the flour in the shape of an S and
touched the tip of her nose.*

*Her eyebrow lifted, and she wiped away the flour. "Roll that
dough."*

Once again, he dropped the ball onto the counter and went about rolling it flat.

"Not too thin, but not too thick either," she instructed.

"That's helpful." He chuckled as he continued to move the rolling pin over the dough.

"No, let me." She took the pin from him and pushed him out of the way with her hip.

He raised his hands in the air as she took over. "I thought you were going to teach me, not do everything for me."

She took a pinch of flour and flicked it at him. "Well, if you did it right, I wouldn't have to take over."

"Well, if you were a better teacher, maybe I would be doing it right." He tossed a small handful of flour at her, leaving a white splotch on the front of her shirt.

Her mouth fell open, and she gave him a devious grin. She scooped a handful of flour and dropped it on top of his head, running her fingers through his hair in the process.

He reciprocated with a handful tossed in her face.

She coughed, and flour puffed out of her mouth at him as she came at him with flour in her grip.

He cracked up laughing, trying to duck away, grabbing her around the waist as he snatched more flour and dropped it down the back of her shirt.

Their laughter filled the room as the white powder flew everywhere, covering them and every surface nearby.

Micah pulled her close, his laugh mingling with hers as he began gently wiping the flour from her eyes, her cheeks, her lips.

She gazed into his eyes as they quieted.

"I love you, Shannon."

Her heart stuttered at his admission. "You do?"

He nodded.

She softly touched his cheek, her thumb brushing the flour from his lips.

He leaned close and kissed her. They'd shared hundreds of kisses before then, but this one surpassed them all. It was also their most unique kiss, with the flour left on their lips becoming pasty and sticky from their kisses.

"Gross!" Shannon pulled away and wiped at her mouth.

Micah burst out laughing. "Not what a guy wants to hear after he tells a girl he loves her."

Shannon giggled and brought her arms up around his neck. "I love you too."

"Remember how your mom made us scrub the entire kitchen, even the parts that weren't covered in flour?" Micah clearly remembered that night as well as she did.

Shannon couldn't pretend she didn't. "We never did get those cookies baked."

He thought for a second. "You're right. We didn't." He smiled over at her. "Totally worth it."

She couldn't smile back. The remembering turned to overwhelming sadness. "I can't do this. I can't spend this whole weekend walking down memory lane with you. It's too hard."

"I don't know why it's so hard for you. *You're* the one who broke up with *me*."

She pressed her lips together.

"I know that look. Don't hold back. Say it."

"You think it was easy for me? I'm not completely devoid of feelings, Micah."

"I'm not saying that. But I think it's usually easier for the *dumper* than the *dumpee*."

He had no idea what he was talking about. That's what she wanted to tell him, but instead she asked, "Can you please take me home now?" She couldn't handle this.

Micah started the car and backed out of the driveway, heading toward Shannon's apartment. They drove in silence for several uncomfortable minutes.

"Does your great aunt still own the house on the lake?" he asked.

"Yes." Nana's sister, Pauline, had lived on the lake for many years, and her house was a special place for the entire family. They spent almost every Fourth of July there for the annual family reunion. They'd have a huge barbecue. Family would come from near and far.

Even Aunt Pauline's neighbors would come by and enjoy good food, great conversation, and a killer view of the fireworks over the lake.

Micah had attended two of those Fourth of July parties with her. One when their relationship was in its infancy—seventeen-year-old kids about to start their senior year of high school. The other a year later when they were in love, graduated, and about to head off to college. They'd shared their last special times together there.

They were so young then. The future was wide open, and they'd had so many dreams. Dreams that would never come true. And it was one of those dreams that had led Shannon to break up with him.

"I loved going to her house with you."

Shannon didn't reply.

"Your family made me feel a part from the first day I met them."

Still, she said nothing.

"You don't really want to talk about this, do you?" Micah asked as he turned onto her street.

"No."

"What if I want to talk about it?" he asked.

"I don't know what good it would do."

"You heard Nana. We should say what we need to say while we have the chance."

"We can't go back in time. We can't change what's happened."

"Would you want that? To change things?" There was a glimmer of hope in his eyes.

"No."

Chapter 6

He knew not to get too close, but he was still disappointed. Not that he'd really let himself believe they could reconcile after one afternoon together, but each moment with her felt so special that a little sliver of hope had snuck through.

Standing in that kitchen with her again, the memories had flooded back—flour flying everywhere, raven hair and sun-kissed skin becoming white and powdery. The look on her face when he told her he loved her for the first time would forever be burned in his memory. Not to mention the kisses that had followed his confession, which had simultaneously filled his heart with joy and lit a fire within him. It was those moments he'd been thinking about today as he ran the line of flour down Shannon's nose. That flame wasn't gone. Far from it. But she'd been quick to douse it, and that stung.

She practically jumped out of the car when they reached her apartment and dashed for her door. She didn't even say goodbye.

Micah stared after her, wondering if he should follow and push her into the conversation he was dying to have. But he didn't move. He remained in his car, eyes fixed on the door to her building.

He started to shift his car into drive, when his phone rang. It was an unknown number, and he almost let it go to voicemail, but he wondered if maybe it was Shannon changing her mind. He tapped the screen to answer just as he realized Shannon didn't have his phone number, but it was already too late.

"Micah, it's Jacqueline. Please don't hang up."

He almost did. He should have, really, but he remained on the line.

"Are you there?" she asked.

"Yes. What do you want, Jacquie?"

"It's been months since we've spoken. You haven't returned any of my calls."

"We broke up." He couldn't help but sound irritated.

"I know. You're with Autumn now. I get it. But we were together for five years, and you don't just get over that. It takes time."

"It's been a year. You should be over it by now."

"I was ready to spend my life with you, Micah. I think it will take more time before I can move on."

He sighed. He did understand, but he wished she would let it go. "Did you need something else?"

She was quiet for a few beats. "I just miss you. I miss your voice. I miss the way you'd hold me and kiss me. I need you, Micah."

"We've been over this. Several times. I've moved on. I'm sorry if that hurts you, but we weren't right for each other. There's a better man out there for you." *One who can put up with your crazy, obsessive, stalker-ish behavior.*

"But I don't want anyone else. I only want you."

"That's not an option. I don't know what else I can say to get you to understand." He'd tried letting her down easy—many times—but she wasn't getting it through her thick skull. He'd tried kindness and understanding, but with each unwanted call or visit to his front door or appearance at his place of employment at all hours of the day and night, he grew more and more impatient with her. It wasn't healthy, this obsessive behavior. She needed to move on. He needed her to. He knew he had to be firm with her. But every time he told her no, he felt cold and unfeeling. Because it was he who had stayed in the relationship longer than he should've for fear of hurting her, even though he knew in his heart he didn't love her enough.

He glanced up at Shannon's apartment window. He understood the pain of being dumped. He knew it all too well, so he got that Jacqueline was hurting. And as much as he longed to be completely free of her, he hated the thought of causing her more heartbreak.

"Can we go to dinner this weekend? Or maybe coffee?" she begged. "I want to catch up. I hate not knowing what's going on in your life."

Micah closed his eyes. His patience was drawing thin. "No, we can't go to dinner, and we can't go to coffee. Autumn wouldn't appreciate that. And you have to let *us* go, Jacqueline. You'll be a much happier person when you do. And God will bring you someone new. Someone perfect for you."

He could hear her sniffling, and he moved the phone away from his ear and let his head drop forward, exasperated and frustrated. He felt completely rude. He hated making girls cry.

"You're the one for me," she whimpered.

"I'm NOT, okay? The sooner you accept that, the better off we'll all be." And then he did the thing he knew he had to do, the thing that made him feel like a world-class jerk. He hung up on her.

Micah dropped his phone into the passenger seat of the car and pulled out of the parking lot. His heart squeezed. He didn't want to leave, and something held him back, like an invisible tether tied between him and Shannon, keeping him from pulling out onto the road. He wanted to put the car in reverse, park it, march up to her door, take her in his arms, and show her how much he still cared about her.

But instead, he reluctantly pulled out and headed to Keely's house.

"Why didn't you tell me Shannon was your wedding photographer?" Micah's tone was sharper than he meant it to be.

The kitchen grew quiet at his question. Keely's family, a couple of her bridesmaids, and Chase looked from Micah to Keely and back.

Keely stared at him, clearly put on the spot. "I forgot the two of you dated. Honestly. I wasn't trying to hide it."

He pressed his lips together. "It would've been nice to have a little advanced warning there."

"I'm sorry," she replied. "Truly."

"Okay." He gave her a little closed-mouth smile, wanting to ease the tension he'd caused.

Everyone went back to their own conversations, munching on chips and salsa, sipping their drinks.

Keely moved to where Micah stood in the entrance of the kitchen. "Was it wrong of me to ask you to drive her home?"

"No, but if you're trying to get us back together, I don't think you'll have any luck."

"Oh?" Keely raised an eyebrow. "You don't sound so sure. Did you talk about it?"

"Not really." Micah wandered over to the kitchen island, grabbed a chip, and dunked it into the salsa. He took a bite and immediately started coughing. "Hot!"

"Yeah, read the label, lightweight. Extra hot." Chase laughed and pointed at the other bowl. "*This* is the mild salsa." He rifled around in the fridge and came back with a glass of milk.

Micah coughed a little more and took a couple swigs of milk to calm the burning in his mouth. "Thanks." He swiped away the milk mustache.

Chase chuckled. "You are such a wimp."

Micah punched him in the arm.

"I didn't realize Shannon our photographer was Shannon your ex." Chase rubbed his arm. "She's the one you were all moody over when we first got to college, right?"

Micah glared at him. "Thanks. Why don't you announce it to everyone?"

Chase shrugged. "I think I just did."

"It's not too late for me to back out of this whole best man thing, ya know."

"Hey," Chase patted him on the back. "You wouldn't do that to me, would you?"

"Keep making me the butt of your jokes and you'll see."

Chase walked through the kitchen and out the french doors onto the back deck, motioning for Micah to follow. "So, it's the same girl, right? The one you were in love with when you got to Liberty? The one who broke your heart?"

"The same." His heart ached just thinking about those first months in Virginia. A future without Shannon had seemed so bleak. He'd been hesitant to leave Michigan without her, but he couldn't

45

stay home either. He wouldn't have been able to stand it, knowing she was so close and didn't want to be with him anymore. So he had gone. And Virginia had been the right choice. He had moved on as best he could—playing baseball, earning his degree, and landing a great job. The life he ended up living looked entirely different than the one he'd imagined. Not that it was bad. But Virginia was supposed to be a temporary stop along his journey before moving back to Michigan. He hadn't expected to settle down there.

"Was it awkward seeing her again?" Chase asked.

Micah thought about that and shook his head. "It felt good just being with her, but it was hard. I loved her so much."

Chase patted him on the back.

"I guess she just didn't love me as much as I loved her."

"You guess?"

"I still don't fully understand what went wrong. We were happy one week and then the next it was like somebody flipped a switch. She went from being so excited for our future together to telling me we were done."

"Yeah, I remember you telling me a little about that back then."

"I tried to get her to talk about it today."

Chase's brow lifted. "How'd that go over?"

"About how you'd imagine. She didn't want to rehash the past."

"I'm sorry, man."

Micah waved him off. "I'll just have to suck it up and get through this weekend and try not to be too close to her, because I'll tell ya, man, it's torture." He was going to have a hard time keeping his distance, because when she was in the room, all he wanted was to be near her. "She's still so beautiful ... and she smells so good."

Chase snickered and turned his attention to a little towheaded girl and boy running around the back yard.

Micah watched them play tag. "Cute kids."

"Flower girl and ring bearer," Chase replied. "Keely's niece and nephew. Her sister's kids."

"Ah. I can picture little Chases and Keelys running around this yard one day." His heart tugged a little at the thought of having his own kids one day. He'd imagined kids with Shannon so many times. They'd talked about it. A lot. Micah shook his head, trying to erase the thought of Shannon holding a baby. All the things they had dreamed about kept coming to the forefront of his mind. He hadn't expected this weekend to drag his emotions through the wringer. He was sure he would be a mess and probably need some serious therapy by the time Chase and Keely said "I do."

"When's Autumn coming?" Chase asked.

"Friday for the rehearsal."

"Does she know about Shannon?"

"She knows a little." Autumn didn't know much about his life before Virginia. She knew where he was from and that he was raised by his aunt because his parents had died when he was a baby. But he hadn't told her much about his relationship with Shannon because it didn't really matter. It was in his past. His old life. It had no bearing on the relationship he had with Autumn.

"That could be awkward."

Micah shook his head. "Autumn's cool. We know where we stand, and her meeting someone from my past isn't going to change that."

"I hope you're right."

"I am." Micah was confident in the mutual respect and admiration he and Autumn had for each other.

"I like Autumn." Chase leaned against the railing and continued to watch the kids.

"So do I."

Chapter 7

Shannon paced her apartment. She had lied when she told Micah she needed rest for tomorrow. It was the only excuse she could think of. She hadn't been lying about backing up the photos, but that hadn't taken her long at all. And now she was alone with her thoughts. Alone with the memories.

She stared over at the clock. 7:22 p.m. They would've been at dinner by now. They'd be catching up on each other's lives, telling each other stories about all the things they'd missed over the past ten years. Maybe they would take a walk together. Their hands would accidentally brush against each other. He would let his fingers slide along the inside of her palm the way he always had, not holding her hand, simply caressing and sending little shivers up her arm. Then he'd drive her home and walk her to the door. He'd lean closer as she moved to go inside. He'd stop her with a kiss and press her up against the door, kissing her until she was dizzy. Maybe she'd invite him in, and they'd end up on her couch, making out until they had to stop or they would take things too far.

She threw herself onto said couch and buried her face in the cushion, groaning loudly. Why? Why did he have this effect on her?

Today had been too much. Too much Micah. Too much of his closeness. Too many memories.

She hated the look on his face when she told him she didn't want to change things. It was another lie, of course, but they couldn't go back. Her situation was still the same, and it wouldn't change. But the more time she spent with him, the more the regret weighed heavy on her.

She rolled onto her back and stared up at the swirly texture on the ceiling. Her mind reeled as she replayed the day. Maybe she should've just talked to him like he'd wanted. Maybe if she explained herself, told him the real reason she broke up with him, he would understand. Micah had never been anything but kind and caring and honest with her. Maybe now, after so much time had passed, he would understand why she did what she did. Maybe he wouldn't hold it against her.

The thought made her stomach flutter with nerves. She'd only seriously considered telling him once before—four years ago. On a visit to Aunt Pauline's, she'd discovered some old pictures of her and Micah, which had spurred buried feelings, filling her with doubt and regret, and led her to look him up on Facebook. The disappointment at seeing a picture of him with his arms around a beautiful blonde girl had crushed her, and she'd closed the browser and cried herself to sleep.

But could she tell him now? Should she? After all this time? If only she could go back and tell her eighteen-year-old self not to make such a rash decision.

Her fingertips skimmed over the small ridge of scarred skin on the left side of her abdomen. She shook her head. *Ridiculous.* She couldn't tell him. It wouldn't make a difference anyway.

His happiness had always been the most important thing to her. She wanted him to have the best life he was meant to have, and it seemed like he was. He was happy and thriving in Virginia. He had Autumn and the perfect job. She would've held him back from getting everything he ever wanted, and telling him now would only cause unnecessary pain. For both of them.

She needed to focus on the areas of her life she could control. She and Jamie were set to hear from Vernon, the owner of the building where Simon had his studio, by the end of the week, and then they would be moving their stuff into the space. Her own photography studio in East Grand Rapids. Life hadn't turned out exactly as she thought it would, but at least she'd get to live out one of her dreams.

She wandered to her desk and plopped down in front of her computer to work on a few of the brunch photos. Almost the first picture that popped up was of Micah and Chase laughing. She clicked the *X* in the corner of her Photoshop program and walked away from the computer, trying to escape him.

Part of her didn't want to.

She paced some more. The idea of telling him still floating around in her mind. She returned to her desk and grabbed her phone, speed-dialing Jamie. She'd know how to talk her down from the ledge.

"Hey," Jamie answered on the fourth ring. "What's up?"

"Nothing."

"How was the brunch today?" Jamie asked.

"My ex-boyfriend is the best man."

Jamie started laughing. "You're kidding."

Shannon could hear music and laughter in the background. "Where are you?"

"I'm at a club with some friends."

"Oh, sorry. I didn't mean to interrupt the fun."

"No worries. Tell me about the best man."

"It's a long story. I'll tell you about it later."

"No way. I'm coming over."

"You don't have to. I'll be going to bed soon anyway." Jamie's cackle was so loud, Shannon had to hold the phone away from her head.

"In bed by seven-thirty? You're twenty-eight, not eighty-eight."

"Maybe I'm tired."

"I'll be there in thirty minutes." Jamie abruptly hung up.

Shannon felt bad for tearing her away from her evening with friends, but she knew there was no talking Jamie out of it now. Once she set her mind to something, she did it. It was one of the things she loved about Jamie. She was also fiercely loyal to her friends. She would give a kidney if one of her friends needed it.

Sure enough, thirty-three minutes later, Jamie showed up at the door to her apartment building, pressing the button to be buzzed in.

"I stopped for necessities." She came bearing two pints of Blue Bunny ice cream—strawberry for herself and sugar-free chocolate for Shannon.

"You are my hero." Shannon snatched the bag of deliciousness out of her hand and went straight to the kitchen for spoons.

The girls settled in on the couch, and Shannon filled Jamie in on all the events of the day. "I shouldn't have taken him to my parents' house. There are just too many memories there, and I knew that. I knew it would dredge stuff up, but I did it anyway, like some kind of idiot." She devoured a huge scoop of ice cream. "I think maybe a part of me wanted to feel bad today, because of how badly I hurt him all those years ago. Punishing myself seemed like the right thing to do."

Jamie narrowed her eyes. "That happened a long time ago. Is he the kind of guy who would hold a grudge?"

"Not really. But he tried to bring it up. He wanted to talk about it, and I told him it wouldn't do any good. I blew him off."

"Why?"

"Because I'm not sure if I should tell him the truth or not."

"The truth about?"

"Why I broke up with him."

Jamie set the pint of ice cream on the end table and turned to face Shannon. She tucked her magenta-streaked brown hair behind her ears and rubbed her palms together. "Okay, this is gonna be good. Lay it on me."

"I'd rather not talk about it."

"Maybe you need to if it's still eating you up ten years later."

Shannon breathed in deeply and let out a heavy sigh. Only her family knew the reason. "I promise to tell you about it sometime, but for now, I just need you to talk me out of telling him."

"Okay, whatever you do, don't tell him."

"Okay."

"It would be a disaster." She took a bite of ice cream.

Shannon nodded. "Right. It would."

"It could bring up a lot of painful feelings."

"Yes. Keep talking. This is working."

Jamie eyed her. "Or …"

"What?"

"It could bring up other kinds of feelings. The really good kind." Jamie raised her eyebrows up and down.

"Jamie!"

51

"I'm sorry, but whatever it is, I say tell him."

"Not helping. Not good."

"It can't make things worse, right? You broke up years ago. And if he's still hung up on you, maybe knowing will help him to move on." Jamie tilted her head and gave Shannon a pointed look. "If that's what you want him to do."

"You suck at this."

"Sorry. What can I say? You've been single for as long as I've known you. You need some action." Jamie picked up the ice cream again and dug in.

Shannon rolled her eyes. She and Jamie could not have been more different when it came to guys.

It wasn't like Shannon hadn't tried to date after Micah left. She'd been on dates and had a couple brief relationships, but none ever lasted. They just weren't Micah.

"On to a completely different—but very exciting—topic ..." Jamie slurped ice cream from her spoon. "Vern wants to meet with us on Friday at eleven o'clock." She bounced a little on the cushion. "Can you believe it? Our own studio space."

"I know. I could kiss Simon for marrying Maggie and opening that shop with her in Hastings."

"I'd kiss Simon." Jamie winked.

"Maggie might have something to say about that."

Jamie laughed. "They're so cute together. I knew something was going to happen with them after Vegas."

Shannon thought back to the Professional Wedding Photographers Convention they had all attended together. "Remember how much Maggie disliked him, and then we saw them kissing on the dance floor."

"Disliked him, indeed." Shannon giggled.

"Well, I'm not sad he left the space empty for us. His loss is our gain." Jamie held her hand up in the air, and they high fived.

Talking about it made Shannon giddy. She couldn't wait to make the space their own and start bringing people in for meetings and photo sessions. This was going to open up her business to lots of new clientele, and she couldn't wait to meet them all.

"Who was at the club with you?" Shannon still felt bad for pulling her away.

"A few friends from college."

"Oh, I was afraid maybe I dragged you away from a date." Shannon wasn't sure how Jamie found the time to date with her busy photography schedule, but she was often out with this guy or that.

"I'm saving myself for your brother," she replied with a wink.

It was no surprise that Jamie liked Duncan. The two of them had always been flirtatious, but that's all it had ever been. Duncan dated occasionally. No one very serious, though. With all his traveling, he seemed to befriend women wherever he went, but he apparently wasn't ready to settle down yet.

"Is he home from Colorado yet?" She seemed a little more interested than usual.

Shannon shook her head. "He gets in late tomorrow night."

"This is one of the longest stretches he's been gone."

"I think he was away for three months once. Why? Do you miss him?" Teasing her about her crush on Duncan was the norm.

"I'm waiting here with open arms." She batted her eyelashes and smiled, but Shannon thought she saw a hint of sadness there as well.

"Not sure my brother knows that. If he did, he would probably rush back right away."

Jamie looked at her hopefully. "Ya think?"

Shannon's eyebrow raised. "I thought we were discussing me and my Micah problem."

"Right. Micah. Didn't we decide already?"

"You did."

"No, seriously, Shannon, don't listen to me. If you think it would be a mistake to tell him, don't do it."

Shannon felt even more confused than she had before.

"Do you want me to come along to the rest of the wedding events and help? I have an engagement session tomorrow night and a wedding on Saturday, but I could be there for the shower and the rehearsal."

"You would do that?"

"Of course."

Working with friends wasn't always the best idea, but the two of them made a perfect team and knew each other so well by now that Jamie didn't need much instruction. She knew what to do and where to be and who she should be photographing without being told. That's why it made so much sense for them to share a studio space together. Plenty of growth and amazing collaborations were in their future, and Shannon couldn't wait.

"I really could use someone there for moral support."

"Consider it done."

"Like I said ... my hero."

Chapter 8

An afternoon bridal shower the day before the rehearsal was an uncommon occurrence, but rather than ask guests to travel to Michigan twice, they opted for this week when everyone would already be in town for the wedding. Keely's shower was exactly what Shannon expected it to be—quaint, elegant, and inviting. Everything was bright and crisp—white linen tablecloths and napkins, white chairs, white balloons with white ribbons—which made the vibrant pink, purple, and fuchsia hydrangeas and roses in the center of each table pop. The napkin rings had a floral print matching the colors in the bouquets. The invitations to the shower itself were white with the same floral print border. And when Shannon moved into the kitchen to photograph the buffet, she noticed the plastic plates also had a floral border in the same colors. Their attention to detail was impeccable.

"These should've been china." Chase's mother, Georgia, pointed to the plates, as if she was apologizing.

"I think they're lovely," Shannon replied. "Everything looks so nice together."

Georgia let out a little harrumph. "Every couple should have a nice set of fine china." It was clear she didn't approve of the choices Keely's mother and sister had made for the shower.

The Penningtons were wealthy and felt like southern royalty to Shannon, though she had no idea what they did that brought them financial success. From what Shannon had gathered at brunch, Chase was very much like his dad—laid back, level-headed, charming. But Georgia had an air of pretentiousness about her and a way of speaking that made Shannon feel uncomfortable and inferior.

Shannon moved around her and focused on the floral detail of the plates before moving to the food. Whenever she photographed an event, she tried her best to capture every minute detail as if it had been her own special day. Pictures of the bride and her guests were a given, but shots of the details were a reminder of all the planning and creativity that went into it. A wedding, a bridal shower, an anniversary party—whatever the case—was a big deal. So much went into bringing an event like this to fruition, and her goal had always been to transport her clients back to their special event with a simple glance at a picture. Just as important as capturing the feeling and emotion of the day were the little things that made it special. Even if those details were simple plastic plates instead of fine china.

She felt Georgia's eyes on her but continued on with her work, trying her best to ignore the condescending gaze. When Georgia finally wandered out of the kitchen, Shannon breathed a sigh of relief.

Once her work in the kitchen was done, she went back to the living room where the tables were set up. As she moved to photograph the long gift table at the front of the room, she nearly dropped her camera. Chase and Micah were standing in the entryway talking with Keely and a couple of her bridesmaids.

Shannon lifted her camera and searched for something—anything—to photograph. She fixed her lens on the flower girl sitting on her mother's lap, pouting. She could feel Micah watching her, and she scanned the room for Jamie, who was busy with her camera in hand. Slowly and deliberately, she moved away from Micah and toward Jamie.

"Hey," Jamie said from behind her camera. "Do we get food at this gig? Whatever is in that kitchen smells so good, my stomach is growling louder than a grizzly bear." She started to laugh to herself, but then noticed Shannon's face. "What's wrong?"

Shannon subtly tilted her head in Micah's direction.

Jamie not-so-nonchalantly looked his way, then back, like she hadn't looked over at him on purpose.

"Subtle." Shannon scrunched up her nose.

"So, that's him, huh? Why are guys at a bridal shower?"

"I have no idea." She thought this would be a fun day with Keely and the girls. If she had known Micah would be there, she could've mentally prepared.

"Don't look now, but he's coming over here." Jamie barely got the words out before he was standing beside them.

"Hey," Micah said.

"Hello." Shannon tried to act aloof, like she couldn't care less that he was there.

"Who's your friend?" he asked.

"Micah, this is Jamie. Jamie, this is Micah."

Micah's eyes widened. "If you ever give up photography, you could totally work in radio."

Shannon's brow furrowed.

"You said that so fast, you could be one of those speed-talking radio announcers that do the disclaimers after the car ads. 'See dealer for details.'"

Jamie laughed and held her hand out to shake Micah's hand. "You're funny."

Shannon wasn't amused.

"Nice to meet you, Jamie."

"You too, Micah. I've heard so much about you."

Shannon gave her a look.

"You have?" Micah looked to Shannon then back at Jamie. "Should I be afraid?"

"Oh, I don't think you have anything to worry about. Shannon would never say a bad word about anyone. She's just that sweet and kind and—"

"Why are you here?" Shannon cut her off.

He appeared wounded. "We just stopped by for a few. We're not staying."

"Good." She could not concentrate with him around, and she needed to focus on work, not how good he looked at the moment.

"Can we talk?" he asked. "Just for a minute."

"I'm working, Micah."

"I know. It'll only take a minute."

She sighed and nodded reluctantly. Her eyes pleaded with Jamie to get her out of this, but Jamie simply shrugged and went back to taking pictures.

Some hero she was.

Micah led her to the kitchen and through the sliding doors onto the deck. She tried not to stand too close to him.

"Chase was wondering if you could come with us guys tonight and photograph the bachelor party."

Her eyes widened. "They didn't hire me for that."

"I know, but he's doing something a little different for his party, and he would love to have pictures."

She stared at him, waiting for him to fill in the blanks.

"Will you come?"

"I need details, Micah."

"You'll just have to come and see what he has planned. Nobody gets details until they arrive."

She wasn't so sure about this.

"They'll pay you for it, if that's what you're worried about."

"I'm worried about what this is and what to expect when I get there. Like, is it going to be R-rated?"

Micah started laughing. "PG, all the way."

"Okay, I guess."

"Excellent. Thank you." He squeezed her arm before heading back inside.

She could barely move from that spot, and little tingles were moving over her skin leaving the hairs on her arm standing on end. *Ugh! Why can't I escape him even for a day?*

"I'll text you the time and location." He spoke over his shoulder as he entered the house.

"Wait, you don't have my number."

"Keely gave it to me."

Keely. She was going to have words with Miss Cupid before this day was through.

Chase and Micah left minutes later, and the air returned to Shannon's lungs.

Jamie wandered up to her. "You didn't tell me how good-looking Micah is."

One would have to be blind not to see how attractive Micah was, which didn't make staying away from him any easier.

They moved to the side of the room as Keely's mother began to speak.

"Thank you all for coming to celebrate Keely's wedding weekend. The women sitting in this room right now make up several generations who've played a part in making Keely the lovely woman she is today. Through your friendship and encouragement and Godly example, you've helped guide her through life and prepared her for the man she will spend the rest of her life with."

Keely waved her hands in front of her face and blew out slowly. "Mom, we're less than a minute in, and you're making my mascara run already."

The room filled with laughter, and Shannon and Jamie captured every moment they could.

Shannon couldn't help but feel a little choked up herself. She was happy for Keely, but she mourned the life she could've had with Micah. It was too late for them. Too late for her to find that kind of happiness.

She focused with sheer determination on photographing the guests so she wouldn't break down. When her camera fixed on Georgia, there was no mistaking the scowl she wore. Shannon didn't know the woman, but she seemed to be in a perpetual bad mood. It made her wonder what their life was like, what could give this woman such a sour disposition.

Once the meal and gift giving were complete, Shannon waited for the opportune time to speak to Keely. She had to tell her she was mostly done with the day's coverage anyway, but she wanted to talk to her about more than photography.

As she approached, Keely's face lit up.

"Thank you so much for today." Keely threw her arms around Shannon's neck.

"You're welcome," she replied.

"The guys said you're going to the bachelor party with them tonight."

"Yeah, about that ..." Surely Keely knew what it was. "What are they doing?"

Keely shook her head. "Uh-uh. You'll find out. Just dress casual. Jeans or shorts and a t-shirt are fine for this."

Shannon's forehead creased. "Should I be worried?"

"About?"

"I don't know. I don't really like surprises."

Keely giggled. "It's not a stripper, if that's what you're worried about."

"No, but is it something scary, like zip lining, or something silly, like Craig's Cruisers?"

"It'll be fun. Something you've never photographed before. At least I don't think you have."

"Well, tell me what it is, and I'll tell you if I have or haven't."

Laughter was her reply.

"And I hope you aren't trying to play matchmaker for me and Micah this weekend. That's in the past, and we can't go there again."

"I told you, I didn't remember you two dated."

"And he has a girlfriend. Autumn. She's coming this weekend to the wedding."

"I know he does," Keely said.

"And I just can't be the woman he needs. I never will be, so—"

"Maybe I was doing a little bit to push the two of you together," Keely admitted, "and I'm sorry about that. I didn't realize you felt so strongly about this."

"I do."

"All right, then I won't interfere anymore. Consider my matchmaking a thing of the past."

"Thank you."

Keely hugged her again, then went to speak with some of her guests before they left.

"What did you mean by that?" Unbeknownst to Shannon, Jamie had been standing close enough to hear their conversation.

"By what?" Shannon replied.

"You can't be the woman he needs? What does that mean?"

"Nothing."

Jamie shook her head vehemently. "Spill."

"Now is not the time to get into it."

"Fine, but you *will* tell me."

She didn't want to talk about it. She lived it on a daily basis. Every day when she gulped down a kale salad or a green smoothie or ate a handful of walnuts instead of a candy bar, she remembered how her body constantly betrayed her. Every day when she popped that birth control pill, she was reminded of what she would likely never have, what she would never be. And every day, when she looked in the mirror, she saw the face of a woman who would never have the future she and Micah had dreamed about.

Chapter 9

Shannon climbed out of Jamie's car and stared at the brightly painted sign before her. CROSSFIRE WOODS.

"Have fun!" Jamie couldn't stop giggling. "Don't get shot!" she cried as she pulled away.

Paint ball was not something Shannon had photographed before, but she was definitely up to the challenge.

"Shannananana!"

It was a voice long ago heard but never forgotten, and she spun around to see Zeb Daniels jogging toward her. His dark blond hair was still buzzed tight to his head—a little less of it than he used to have. His tall, broad-shouldered stature was the same, but he looked like he'd packed on a few pounds in the last ten years. One thing that hadn't changed at all was his big, comforting grin that made a girl feel like she was the only one in the world. And she bet his hugs were just as tight as they used to be.

He scooped her up and lifted her off the ground with his giant, bear-like arms.

Yep. Exactly the same.

"Zeb! How are you? It's been too long."

He lowered her to the ground and laid his heavy hands on her shoulders. "You look just as pretty as you always did." He leaned in as if to tell her a secret. "Maybe even prettier."

She blushed a little at his sweetness. He had always been that way. There was something about him that made all the girls feel special.

And he meant every word he said. There was absolutely nothing fake or insincere about Zeb Daniels. He was as genuine as a person could get.

"What've you been up to?" she asked.

"I own a sporting goods store up north. Keeps me pretty busy."

"You own it? That's amazing. I'm so happy for you."

"Aw, thanks. It was left to me when my dad died, so it wasn't like I set out to do that with my life."

"Oh, I'm so sorry, Zeb."

He smiled. "Thanks. I'm happy there. It's what I was meant to do."

She glanced down at his hand, curious if he had ever married Charlotte. *No ring.*

"You're wondering if I'm married."

Her eyes shot to his. *Busted.* "I was simply curious if someone helped you up there in that store. Maybe Char—"

"Nope." A shadow of sadness crossed his face for an instant, then his usual grin returned. "Just me. For now." He winked at her.

Zeb had always been flirtatious with her, but they had been such good friends that moving from friends to more hadn't felt right to Shannon.

"So Micah invited you down here for this?" she asked.

He nodded. "I haven't seen him ... well, probably since I last saw you, but we've kept in touch. Facebook and all."

"I think the last time I saw you was the summer after we graduated."

He shook his head. "Dang, has it really been that long?"

"Unfortunately." She turned into him and wrapped an arm around his waist.

His arm draped over her shoulder. "I've missed you, Shorty."

She'd never been one for nicknames, but every name he'd ever called her seemed to suit her. At least when *he* said it. "I've missed you too." She looked around then up at Zeb. "Do you know where everybody is? I haven't seen any of the other guys yet."

He lowered his arm and rotated, pointing to his back. "Hop on! I'll take you to them."

Shannon started laughing.

"Get up here." He bent a little at the knees and held his hands out to the sides to catch her legs.

"Oh, you're serious? I've got camera equipment to carry."

His arms extended to the sides like a coat tree. "Lay it on me."

She laughed again, but did as he asked, looping the straps of her bag and camera over his shoulders.

"Hop on!" He turned his back to her.

She shrugged. "Why not."

Her hands gripped his strong shoulders, and she jumped, squeezing his hips with her legs, his large mitts taking hold under her thighs. She couldn't stop laughing. "Remember that night you guys won districts and you carried me around the football field for like half an hour?"

"Oh man, that night was legendary."

Shannon giggled.

Zeb walked them along a path toward a wooded area until a group of guys came into sight. "Hey, guys! I brought the photographer!" he hollered.

The sight of so many familiar faces—guys she hadn't seen since high school—surprised her. She assumed Micah had invited them since Chase didn't know anyone in the area other than his groomsmen.

Zeb picked up pace and bounced her a little as he moved closer to the group. Some of the guys started whooping and clapping.

When he released her legs and set her on solid ground, her eyes met Micah's. He did not look happy.

"Zeb ... buddy," Micah stuttered. "You made it."

"And I'm gonna kick your butt." Zeb chuckled.

Shannon removed the camera equipment from his arms. "I'll be rooting for ya, Zeb."

He put his arm around her again and squeezed her into his side. "Thanks, Shorty."

She leaned into him, knowing it was bugging Micah.

"Okay, guys! Before we get started ... Shannon is off limits," Chase announced. "Those little balls filled with paint are to go nowhere near her or her photography equipment. Got it?"

"Got it!" several guys replied.

"Let's go!"

The guys broke off into teams and went their separate ways. There were barriers and small buildings set up throughout the woods for the guys to hide in and around.

Shannon did her best to stay on the fringe of all the action, keeping her distance and using zoom lenses to get close, rather than being too near the line of fire.

Every once in a while, she found herself drifting closer, trying to find Micah, wondering what he was thinking earlier when she arrived on Zeb's back. She shook her head and aimed her camera at Zeb, snapping a picture just as the paint ball left the gun.

It looked like fun, and she made a mental note to add paint ball to her bucket list.

By the time the game was almost over, she was giddy to see her photographs. More than a few times, she had released the camera shutter when a paint ball exploded against someone's chest, hoping to freeze the moment forever. She couldn't wait to see what she had captured, so she opened the image viewer on her camera and began cycling back through some of the pictures.

In the midst of looking at her photos, she took a few steps forward, not paying attention to her surroundings, not noticing a player to her right had his sight fixed on one to her left. In that second, something hit her hard in the stomach as she was caught in the crossfire.

Chapter 10

Shannon's scream sent a terrifying chill through Micah's entire body. Her name was in his head, nearly on his lips, when someone else called out to her, and more than one guy ran to her rescue.

"Shannon!" Zeb bolted to her side in two seconds.

Micah yanked the protective mask from his head and ran toward her. She was doubled over, tears streaming down her face, orange paint splattered on her stomach. Her camera lay on the ground, shards of lens glass scattered on the ground next to it.

"Are you all right?" Micah asked.

She held up her hand as she breathed in and out slowly. "It stings," she managed.

"It's all right, sweetie." Zeb rubbed his hand back and forth between her shoulders.

Micah rolled his eyes. He had nothing against Zeb. They'd been friends for a long time. If not for him always hanging out with Shannon in high school, Micah might never have summoned the nerve to approach her. But he couldn't help but be annoyed at Zeb's hands all over her. He fought the urge to yank Zeb's arm away.

Chase must have noticed Micah's eye rolling, because he was smirking.

"What can I do, Shannon?" Micah asked.

"My camera," she mumbled.

"I've got it." Zeb instantly scooped up the camera, kicking the broken glass under a bush. "What should I do with it?"

Shannon was still bent over, and all Micah wanted was to go to her and take her in his arms to comfort her.

She slowly straightened her body to standing. "Who shot me?"

Micah's heart jumped into his throat. He hadn't meant to do it. Zeb had run that direction, and he hadn't seen Shannon until his finger was squeezing the trigger, and by then, it was too late. Two paintballs had left the chamber and flew straight for her.

"Anyone? Anyone? ... Bueller?"

Her mention of *Ferris Bueller's Day Off* normally would've made him laugh, but he didn't feel much like laughing now.

He took one step forward. "I did."

Her mouth fell open.

"It was an accident."

She took the camera from Zeb and began to move away from the woods, gently rubbing her stomach, walking slowly toward the main entrance with Zeb on her heels.

"Zeb!" Micah called after him.

Zeb turned. "Yeah?"

"Let me." Micah dropped his gun and protective gear on the ground next to Chase and caught up to her. "I'm so sorry about your lens, Shannon. I'll replace it."

"Don't bother. I have insurance on my equipment."

"Oh." He was only trying to help.

Her eyes found his. "Are you sure this wasn't revenge?"

His brow furrowed. "For what?"

"For me breaking up with you."

His laughter stopped short when he noticed the serious look on her face. The air felt thick between them, even though the evening temperature was pleasant and mild.

"You think I would purposely shoot you?"

She shrugged. "I don't know. Maybe you wanted to hurt me. It was no easy thing, our breakup. The pain ... well, it can't have gone away completely. I know it hasn't for me."

His face scrunched up when he looked at her again. "Once again, you're acting like the victim when it was *me* who got dumped."

Shannon chewed on her bottom lip as they walked.

He hadn't meant to sound like such a jerk, but it was the truth.

There was no way she could've felt half as bad as he did about their breakup. How could she? She had walked away seemingly unscathed.

She suddenly stopped and stared across the parking lot. "I forgot, I don't have a car here. Jamie dropped me off."

"I can take you home," he offered.

"No, you're here for Chase. You haven't finished your game yet."

"He'll understand."

"Micah, just let me call Jamie," she snapped.

He stepped closer, and he wondered if that scared her, because she took a step back. He took the camera from her hand, feeling pretty awful for breaking the thing that was her livelihood. He tugged the strap until it slid down her arm and rested it over his own shoulder. Without thinking, he reached out and touched the front of her shirt with the back of his fingers.

A little gasp escaped her lips.

His eyes lifted to hers. He hadn't meant anything by it. The vibrant splotch of orange paint on her stomach appeared wet, and he simply wanted to see if it was, that's all. But now he couldn't seem to remove his hand. The heat of her body radiated through her shirt.

"What are you doing?" Her stomach moved in and out as her breathing rate increased.

"I'm sorry I shot you."

He longed to be closer to her. His fingers twitched at the thought of sliding them over her stomach and around her waist, bringing her against him, touching his lips to hers. He'd missed her plenty of times over the years, but he hadn't realized to what extent until that moment.

With his fingers against her stomach, his control was slipping quickly. The desire to kiss her overwhelmed him, but he knew it couldn't happen. He had to step away before he did something he would regret.

Taking a deep breath in through his nose, he dropped his hand and looked down at the ground as he breathed out.

Suddenly, without warning, Shannon stepped close and laid her hand on his chest.

His eyes shot up to hers as every nerve in his body focused in on the place her hand rested.

"I forgive you, Micah."

He swallowed hard, trying to calm his racing heart.

"But I think it's only fair if I get to shoot you too."

"What?" Had he heard her right?

"I think you should let me shoot you." She slid her hand down to his stomach.

He struggled to suppress a groan.

"Right here." She pushed both hands against his stomach, shoving him out of her personal space.

It was just in time, because her touch had nearly caused him to grab hold of her and plant one on those full, sweet lips.

"Come on." She headed toward the woods.

"You're serious?"

"Where's your gun?" she asked.

He stared after her.

She looked over her shoulder at him. "Let's go, Shaw."

He sighed. She wasn't letting this go.

They walked back to the group in silence. He couldn't believe she would actually go through with it. She wasn't that vindictive. Or was she?

Micah laid the camera down on the ground and picked up the gun he'd left lying at Chase's feet. Shannon quickly snatched it from him.

"You don't even know how to shoot—"

She pulled the trigger, coloring a spot on the ground with paint.

"Hold on, and I'll show you how to use it."

Some of the guys moved toward them and gathered to see what was going on.

Zeb came up beside Shannon before Micah had a chance. "You gonna join the game, Shan?"

"Nope. Just a little target practice." She aimed the gun at Micah, and Zeb laid his hand on top of it, lowering it to the ground.

"Don't shoot him at close range like that," he said.

"He shot me. I think I should get to shoot him back."

Zeb moved Shannon backwards, while Micah moved the same distance Shannon had been from him when he accidentally shot her.

"There. *Now* shoot him." Zeb chuckled as he moved behind her.

Micah stood alone and vulnerable, wincing before Shannon even lifted the gun. "Can't I put on my vest?" He pointed to the protective gear by Chase's feet.

"No way! I didn't have one." Shannon giggled as she aimed for Micah. "I'm not a very good aim, by the way."

His arms instinctively crossed in front of his lap, which had everyone laughing.

The end of the gun bobbed up and down with Shannon's laughter.

"Please don't fire while you're laughing," he pleaded.

"You better move your arms, buddy," Chase told him.

"Better my arms than my ability to reproduce."

Shannon's smile disappeared, and she lowered the gun.

Micah suddenly jumped at the sound of a branch snapping under Zeb's foot, which revived the laughter.

"Come on," he pleaded. "Just get it over with."

She raised the gun again, concentrating on her aim.

"Isn't there another way?" Micah asked. "I'm sure we can come up with some—"

Shannon fired and hit him square in the stomach, exactly where he had hit her.

He groaned and grabbed his gut. "Gah, that smarts."

"Oh, well, if it wasn't that bad, maybe I should do it again so you know how bad it was for me." She aimed again.

"No, no, no!" He held his hands out in front of him. "It hurts. It hurts like a son of a gun."

Shannon lowered the gun, but there was no look of satisfaction on her face, only sadness.

Micah rubbed his stomach, hoping the sting would subside quickly. He walked to Shannon and gently gripped her arm.

She looked up at him with a weak smile.

"I'm sorry. I didn't mean to hurt you."

"I know."

He slid his hand down the side of her arm before letting go. It almost felt like she shivered, but maybe it was his imagination. "I'll take you home when you're ready."

She pressed her lips together. "All right. Thanks."

Micah handed the paintball equipment over to Chase and retrieved her camera.

He was on edge as they walked to his car. He needed somewhere to focus this excess tension. Shannon had gotten him all riled up in a way he hadn't been in a very long time. He liked it and he hated it, and he wasn't sure how he was going to endure sitting next to her in a car for half an hour. Being close to her these past two days reminded him of all they once had and how much he wanted it all again.

But if there was one thing he wanted more than anything out of this weekend, it was to get the truth out of her, to finally understand why she'd ended things with him. If she hadn't loved him, he could've lived with that, but he knew that wasn't the truth. He'd always known it. No one could fake the kind of connection they had.

So, what was the truth? Why had she pushed him away? He had to know.

Chapter 11

When Shannon had left home that afternoon, unsure of what to expect, she never would've imagined she'd end up shot. Being shot by Cupid's arrow wasn't completely out of the realm of possibility, thanks to Keely's matchmaking ways, but shot with a paintball? And by Micah, of all people?

Shannon giggled to herself, feeling proud that she'd actually had the guts to shoot him back.

"What's funny?" Micah turned his attention briefly from the road to her face.

She grabbed hold of the front of her shirt then pointed at his and couldn't help the laughter that bubbled up.

He let out a few chuckles. "It's not that funny."

"It's painful, that's what it is. I'm sure I have a nasty bruise."

"Well, so do I."

She laughed again. "We'll have matching bruises."

Micah smiled over at her, then looked back at the road. "Do you mind if we stop at my aunt's on the way? I need to grab clean clothes before I meet up with the guys again."

Shannon shook her head.

Micah's aunt was a quiet woman who kept to herself, which probably had a lot to do with that side of Micah—the side that craved a simple life. She was pleasant and kind, but not extremely affectionate. Micah had learned that from her.

Coming from a family who freely gave hugs—and often—it had taken Shannon a while to get Micah used to that. She had done her best to warm him up, to break through his tough exterior. When they first got together, she initiated all of the hugs. Much prepping was done before they first spent time with her family, because he was assaulted with bear hugs the instant he walked through the door. But he hadn't seemed to mind. He had taken it in stride, and eventually began giving Shannon hugs without being asked. Gosh, she missed his hugs. Over the course of their relationship, he became really good at giving them and even better at knowing exactly when she needed one.

As they turned into the driveway, she spotted his old truck parked beside the garage, which brought about a wave of memories. She was about to mention it, when he jerked the car to an abrupt stop.

Her eyes shot to his. "What was that?"

His gaze was glued to the porch. More specifically, to the woman standing on the porch talking to his aunt.

Shannon didn't get a chance to ask who it was before he flew out the door, striding across the lawn. She climbed out just as he spoke.

"What are you doing here?"

He seemed pretty ticked off. Was it Autumn? It couldn't be. She was supposed to arrive on Friday. Maybe she came early. But why was he so upset about it?

"I thought you'd be happy to see me," the woman replied.

"Micah, you didn't tell me she was coming." His aunt appeared uneasy.

"I didn't know."

Shannon walked hesitantly toward them, and the woman locked eyes with her.

"That's not Autumn." The woman eyed her, giving her a once over.

"No." Micah was short with her.

She was tall and slender. Blonde with blue eyes. Elegant and downright gorgeous. Side by side, the two of them made the perfect couple.

Shannon wondered what their history was. How did he know her? Did they date? She looked familiar. Could she be the girl from the Facebook photo years ago? She wanted to ask so many questions, but

73

the woman was giving her the evil eye. She decided to be the bigger person and walked toward her with extended hand. "Hi, I'm Shannon. And you are?"

"Leaving," Micah answered for her.

The woman shook Shannon's hand. "I'm Jacqueline, Micah's girlfriend."

Shannon's eyebrows lifted, and she looked over at Micah. "How many are there?"

"Ex," Micah corrected her. "She's my ex-girlfriend."

Jacqueline laid a hand on his bicep. "We've been talking, trying to work things out."

He shook his head as he shook her hand off. "*You've* been talking. I told you, I'm ..." His eyes met Shannon's, and he looked pained as he finished the sentence. "I'm with Autumn now."

"It doesn't look like you're with her right now." Jacqueline's eyes moved from Shannon to Micah.

"I don't have to explain myself to you." Micah seemed to have very little patience when it came to this woman.

"Why don't you all come inside, and I'll make you some tea," his aunt said.

"We can't stay, Aunt Sue. I'm here to change and get back to the bachelor party."

Jacqueline's eyebrow raised. "Is she the stripper?"

Shannon's mouth fell open, as did Micah's.

"For the bachelor party," Jacqueline continued. "Is she tonight's entertainment?"

Aunt Sue seemed uncomfortable and wandered into the house mumbling, "I'll put the water on."

The nerve of this woman. Shannon almost walked away right that instant, but then another thought came to mind, and she went with it before she really considered the consequences.

Sauntering closer to Micah, she tugged the right sleeve of her shirt down off of her shoulder. She slid her arms around his waist from the side, leaning into him with her lips close to his neck. "So what if I am," she breathed in the sexiest voice she could muster.

Shannon felt Micah tense up beside her, and his Adam's apple raised as he swallowed hard. All she'd meant to do was give this woman a hard time, which seemed to be working by her shocked expression. But she knew Micah. After all this time, she still knew him. And she could tell when he was affected by her. *What have I done?*

Nervously, Shannon giggled and pulled away. "Just kidding."

Micah cleared his throat, struggling to speak. "Shannon is not a stripper. She's an old friend." The look he gave Shannon was so intense, it made her stomach flutter. Yep, she had affected him. "Can you give us a few minutes?"

Shannon nodded. "Sure." She went inside to talk to his aunt, wishing she could be a fly on the wall to hear the conversation they were about to have.

"It's so nice to see you again, Shannon." Aunt Sue smiled warmly at her. "How are you, dear?"

"I'm doing well. How are you?"

"Very well, thank you." She went about filling up the teapot with water and placing it on the stovetop. "How's your photography going?"

"It's going well. I'm pretty busy, which is a good thing. My friend and I are planning to open up our own studio in East Grand Rapids soon."

"Oh, how nice for you. Micah's very proud of you for making your dream come true, you know?"

She was taken aback. He hadn't been close with his aunt growing up and had always found it difficult to confide in her. "That's sweet of him."

Shannon could hear voices from the front porch, but they didn't carry like she hoped. She couldn't make out anything they were saying. So, instead, she decided to probe for answers.

"How long were Micah and Jacqueline together?" she asked.

"Oh, about five years, I think. Since senior year of college." She leaned closer as if they could hear her speaking. "She's a pretty girl, but I never thought she was good enough for our Micah. He was pretty broken up after you …" She paused as if she wasn't sure she should've said that. "I was always holding out hope for the two of you."

Yet another comment that caught her off guard. When she and Micah were together, Aunt Sue hadn't seemed the least bit interested in them or their relationship. They'd been wrapped up in each other and senior year activities, and since he wasn't close with his aunt, they'd spent a good portion of their time with Shannon's family. But seeing her now after all this time, Shannon could tell she had misjudged her. Sue truly cared for her nephew and had obviously cared about the two of them together. Clearly, Micah's relationship with her had changed, and Shannon wondered if he'd confided in her after the breakup. It still ached deep inside knowing she'd left him heartbroken over her, but it gave her some comfort thinking his aunt might've been there for him to lean on.

Shannon returned to her previous line of thought. "Why did you think she wasn't good enough for him?"

"He wasn't the same with her. I could tell she didn't make him as happy as he could be." She shook her head. "Plus, there's something a little off about her."

"What do you mean?"

The door opened then, and Micah walked in with Jacqueline following behind.

"You can't stay here," he muttered.

She waved him off. "That's up to your aunt."

He looked seriously agitated as he swept through the space and down the hallway to his old bedroom.

Jacqueline settled in to the chair next to Shannon as if she owned the place. "Would it be an imposition if I stayed here for the night? It wasn't a planned trip, really, and I have no place to go. I just had to see my Micah."

This girl would not take no for an answer. It was obvious Micah did not want her there.

"I'm not sure that would be a good idea," Aunt Sue replied. "I'm sorry, dear."

"Oh." Jacqueline's cheeks colored, maybe from a blush or maybe from anger. It was hard to tell. "All right, well, do you know of any nearby hotels that aren't too expensive?"

"Just go home," Micah ordered as he entered the room and motioned for Shannon to follow.

Shannon stood and walked to Aunt Sue, leaving her with a hug. "It was so wonderful to see you."

"You too, Shannon. Don't be a stranger." She smiled at her genuinely.

"I won't." And she meant it.

Micah walked to his aunt, leaned down, and gave her a kiss on the cheek, then whispered something into her ear, to which she responded with a knowing smile.

"We'll talk more tomorrow," Jacqueline called as they headed toward the front door.

"I'm busy tomorrow," Micah called back over his shoulder. "Chase's wedding, remember?"

Once they were safe in the confines of the car, away from his ex, Shannon looked at him. "What was that?"

"She really wasn't like that when we were together. I swear." He started the engine.

"What did you say to your aunt?" She was beyond curious.

He smirked. "I told her under no circumstances to let Jacquie stay here, and if she didn't leave on her own within the hour, to call me."

"Would she try to stay, even though you both said no?"

He rested his arm across the back of her seat as he backed up. "What do you think?"

She didn't need any more answer than that. Micah's ex *was* a little off as his aunt had put it. "Maybe you need a restraining order."

"I don't want to take it that far. I thought she'd leave me alone when Autumn and I started dating, but every once in a while, she calls or shows up and presses the issue."

"But she's as gorgeous as a supermodel. She could get any guy she wants. Why is she stuck on you?"

He looked wounded.

"I mean, you are quite a catch, but she's got to know she could easily find someone else. Right?"

He stared straight ahead at the road.

"Right?"

"I was going to propose."

Shannon laughed in spite of herself.

He wore the most serious of expressions.

"Oh, she's the one you wanted to marry?"

"Like I said, she wasn't like this before. But I realized I wasn't ready, that she wasn't the one I wanted to spend my life with." He paused and gazed at her for a moment before continuing. There was so much behind his eyes, so much she knew he was holding back, and it made Shannon's heart ache. "When I finally told her, it was like she was in denial. She wouldn't hear it. She went about like it hadn't happened, like I hadn't just broken up with her. I thought moving on would make it sink in, but it hasn't. Her showing up here is the last straw. I don't know what to do anymore."

"Maybe you'll have to actually get married for her to finally take the hint."

His eyes found hers again. "I'm not ... that is, Autumn and I aren't that serious."

"Yet." Shannon avoided eye contact.

He didn't say anything to the contrary, and the car remained silent.

The idea of him marrying Autumn or Jacqueline or any other woman felt like a knife driving straight into her heart. But she had no right to be upset or hurt or feel anything if he chose to marry someone else, because *she* had left him.

It could never happen for them anyway. It was a fact she had come to terms with a long time ago. Or so she thought.

"I'd try the restraining order if I were you." She laughed it all off, because if she didn't, the tears that were now burning behind her eyes might reveal her true feelings.

Chapter 12

Standing on the porch of his childhood home with his two ex-girlfriends had been beyond awkward. He could only imagine how strange it would be for Shannon once Autumn arrived tomorrow. Girlfriends, ex-girlfriends, almost-fiancées everywhere.

They didn't speak after the restraining order comment, and he drove straight to her apartment and shut the car off.

"Thanks for the lift." She climbed out of the car, and he followed. "You don't have to walk me in."

"Let me help with your equipment, at least." He grabbed her bag and the broken camera, and she reluctantly allowed him.

Once they reached her door, she took the bag and camera from him and set them just inside on the floor, not letting him come in. "Interesting day."

He chuckled. "Yeah, to say the least."

"I'm sorry you have to deal with your crazy ex-girlfriend."

"Thanks for trying to be nice to her today. I'm sorry she called you a stripper."

Shannon let out a little giggle, which grew into a laugh, then full-blown laughter.

It didn't seem so funny at the time, but now, her laughter was contagious and soon they were both cracking up over it. And it felt really good. So many years had passed since they'd laughed like this together, and it did things to him. Things he wasn't expecting. But that's how it had always been with her. They could be doing the most mundane things and a look, a laugh, a touch would ignite something inside him that he had no control over when it came to her.

He thought back to Jacquie's stripper comment and Shannon's response. "You ... uh, sure started to play the part there for a second, though." Speaking of igniting a fire within. The sight of her bare shoulder, the feel of her chest against his side, her breath against his neck. Had she been trying to kill him? Because she'd been close to succeeding.

Her laughter caught in her throat. "Yeah, sorry about that. I was insulted, and I wanted to mess with her." She made eye contact with him then.

"I didn't say I didn't like it." *Could I be any more obvious?*

"Uh ..." A nervous laugh escaped her lips. "Well, have fun with the guys tonight." She added a playful punch to the stomach.

He groaned. "Oh, come on."

She gripped his arm. "Sorry. I forgot."

"You forgot you shot me?" He lifted his shirt to see if a bruise had formed yet. The site was red and turning purple in a halo around the point of impact.

She gasped at the sight, and her lip stuck out in an apologetic pout.

He dropped his shirt and fixed his eyes on her pouty lip, before pressing his closed fist against her stomach, as if he was going to reciprocate.

She took a step back. "Don't you dare." And then she lifted the bottom edge of her shirt until her own halo-shaped bruise was revealed, all purple and blue against smooth creamy skin.

What caught his attention wasn't the bruise, but two small scars on either side of her stomach, both less than an inch in size.

"What happened here?" He touched one of them with his index finger, and she yanked her shirt down.

"Nothing. Just a scratch."

He raised an eyebrow at her. He'd seen enough knee injuries on the baseball team to know those were incision scars. "Was it something serious?"

She shook her head, clearly not wanting to talk about it.

"Are you sure?" His insides twisted as his mind raced through the list of ailments and diseases that could require surgery. Wondering what had caused those scars was enough to drive him crazy with worry, and the longing to protect her overwhelmed him.

"I'm fine, Micah."

He searched her face, but she wouldn't make eye contact, so he gently tapped his knuckle to her stomach, hoping to lighten the mood. She didn't respond at first, and he wasn't sure she even felt it. But he felt her—soft and warm—and it heated him all over.

"Now we're even," he teased.

She reached out, brushing her fingertips against the back of his hand. "Ouch?" Her lips turned up in a playful smile.

He moved the backs of his fingers against the smooth skin of her palm and along the inside of her wrist. He could've sworn he felt her heart racing as he skimmed across the vein there. His was beating in the same quick rhythm.

"Don't you have to meet Chase now?" Her voice was nearly a whisper.

"Mhmm." His hand moved around her wrist, along the outside of her arm, and up to her face, where he brushed his fingertips along the side of her cheek with a feather-like touch.

She reached up and laid her hand over his.

He leaned closer. Those eyes. That face. His forehead rested against hers, the scent of her seizing his senses.

"Micah, please," she breathed.

"Please, what?" What did she want him to do? Hold her? Touch her? Kiss her?

"Please stop," she answered.

Surely not that.

"Nothing's changed, Micah," Shannon spoke softly. "And I won't let you jeopardize your relationship with Autumn just because we're still attracted to each other."

"You're still attracted to me?" He smiled down at her.

"That was never the problem," she replied.

He took her upper arms in his hands and looked her in the eyes. "Then tell me, what *was* the problem?"

"I told you, I wasn't ready. I couldn't go to Virginia with you. We were going down different paths."

81

"We could've made long distance work. I wanted to make it work. Why didn't you?"

"We were just kids. What did we know?"

He shook his head. "Don't do that. Don't downplay what we had. We knew we loved each other and wanted to spend the rest of our lives together. We knew how lucky we were, how rare it was for us to find each other so young. We knew it back then, and we know it now."

Shannon stared down at the welcome mat.

"Look at me," he whispered.

She shook her head.

He touched under her chin, urging her to give him her attention.

When she did, he found tears pooling in her eyes.

"What is it? What aren't you saying?" he pleaded, dying to know her thoughts.

She blinked, and a tear slid down her cheek. "I knew you'd be happier if you left and never looked back."

"How could I ever be happy without you?" His fingers traveled over her shoulders, resting on either side of her neck. "I've been looking back for ten years."

"Well, maybe you shouldn't anymore. Maybe you should look forward to your future—maybe with Autumn. Definitely *not* with Jacqueline," she said with a smirk.

Micah knew she was trying to deflect the conversation, but he found nothing amusing in what she was saying. "What if I want a future with *you*?"

Her eyes instantly filled with tears again. At first, he thought maybe they were happy tears. Maybe it was what she had wanted him to say all along. Until she stepped back out of his arms and shook her head.

"I can't be your future, Micah." She wiped at her cheeks as she moved into her apartment to close the door between them.

He kicked his foot out in time to stop it from closing. "Shannon," he pleaded.

"I'm sorry, Micah." She lowered her head as she shut him out. Out of her apartment. Out of her heart.

Laughter and conversation surrounded the bonfire, but Micah wasn't in the mood for either. He stared at the flames licking upward toward the sky, unable to focus on anything but the pain. It was as if his heart had been ripped out of his chest for a second time. And by the same person. He was an idiot for letting her do it again. He'd started to let hope in only to be crushed all over again. Why couldn't she be his future? He was no closer to the answer to that question than before.

"Cheer up, friend." Chase patted him on the back.

"Easy for you to say," Micah responded. "You're about to marry the love of your life in less than two days. The love of mine just obliterated me ... again."

"Oh man, I'm so sorry. What can I do?"

Micah waved him off. "Just be happy. Be the happiest son of a gun ever. At least one of us will."

"Hey, I don't know what went down today, but she's not the only girl you're ever gonna love."

"Yeah, she is."

Chase tilted his head to make eye contact. "So, where does that leave Autumn then?"

If only Chase understood the dynamics of his relationship with Autumn—maybe arrangement was a better term for it. She had been a good friend to him through college—the best—always there for him when things weren't going well with Jacqueline. A true confidante. And he loved her. Of course he did. But the love he had for Autumn was on a different spectrum from the love he had for Shannon.

If he could explain that to Chase, he would. But nobody knew the true nature of their relationship—they'd agreed to keep it to themselves—so he didn't explain. He simply shrugged his shoulders.

"She's a great girl, Micah. Don't ignore what's right in front of you for someone from your past who obviously doesn't want you."

Those last three words broke him. He stood, unable to talk about this anymore. "I'll see you for breakfast tomorrow."

"Oh, man, it's still early. Stay."

"I can't. I need to sleep this off." He said it knowing full well he wouldn't get a wink.

Micah said his goodbyes and drove home. He wondered what Shannon was doing at the moment. Was she as upset about their conversation as he was?

He pulled up to his aunt's house. Jacqueline's vehicle was gone. *Thank goodness.* At least one thing had turned out right this evening.

When his back hit the bed, tears burned hot in his eyes and slipped down his temples onto the pillow. It hurt as much now as it had ten years ago. Why? Why couldn't she be his future? There was more to this. More she wasn't telling him. Who cares if she couldn't go to Virginia with him? Why hadn't she been willing to make it work? After everything—all their time together, their dreams, their friendship and love—what had changed so suddenly?

Chapter 13

Micah, there's something I need to tell you.

That's all she would've had to say when he saw her scars. She hadn't meant to lift her shirt like that. Or had she? Maybe, deep down, she'd wanted him to see the scars so she'd have to come clean. If ever there was a perfect time to tell him, that would've been it. The words had been right there on the tip of her tongue. But she hadn't done it. The moment had come and gone.

Sleep alluded her that night, and the hours crawled by, as illuminated by the digital alarm clock at her bedside. Her heartbeat hadn't slowed down since Micah left. She'd wanted him to kiss her so badly. How many times had she imagined them together again? It had taken all of her willpower to tell him to stop.

She was the worst person in the world for putting that same broken look on his face after all these years. And she hated herself for it. Hurting him again was the last thing she wanted, which reinforced that she needed to keep the truth to herself.

Looking like a zombie, Shannon rolled out of bed at daybreak and pulled out the coffeemaker. Normally, she avoided caffeine, but after the sleepless night, she knew she'd need it to get her through the events of the day.

The first sip tasted glorious. How long had it been since she'd allowed herself coffee? She took another sip and a sudden flurry of emotion hit her out of nowhere. Tears filled her eyes, and she let them fall, a few sliding down her cheek and into her mug, leaving ripples across the surface of the dark liquid.

She was tired. And not only from lack of sleep. She was weary of living life the way she had for nearly a decade. If only she didn't have to pay such close attention to the foods she put into her body. If only she could go crazy and eat anything she wanted and drink a gallon of coffee and ... Cherry Coke ... oh, how she missed Cherry Coke ... and lasagna. Her mouth began to water. She missed her mom's lasagna. Whenever Mama made it, Shannon would allow herself one small bite, but what she really wanted was to eat a plateful and seconds if she felt like it. Some days, she longed to be ... normal.

Her phone rang then, and she wiped the tears away before she answered.

"Hello?"

"I'm home, and I brought a surprise." Duncan loved buying gifts and souvenirs for his family on all of his many travels.

"Welcome home!" It was so good to hear her brother's voice, and he had perfect timing.

"What are you doing today?" he asked. "I can't wait to show you."

He was usually excited to give gifts, but he sounded even more so this time.

"I'm meeting with Jamie and the guy who's leasing us Simon's old studio this morning, then Keely's final dress fitting, then rehearsal tonight."

"So, the wedding's tomorrow, huh?"

"Yeah, but I'll see you Sunday. Lunch at Mom and Dad's. Sì?"

"Sì." He sounded disappointed.

"What is it?"

"Nothin'. I just missed my sister."

"You mean Sophia?"

He snickered. "I can't ever get that girl on the phone. She's far too busy in the glamorous world of fashion to call her brother."

Shannon had to agree. She was happy their sister had found what she wanted to do with her life, but she couldn't remember the last time she'd spoken to Sophia.

"I'm sorry to cut this short," Shannon said, "but I really have to get ready for this meeting."

"No problema."

"See you Sunday."

"Okay."

"And D, I'm glad you're home."

"Me too."

Duncan was her best friend. He had always been her touchstone, keeping her grounded, reminding her what was important. In the days before and after her breakup with Micah, he'd been so supportive. He knew the whole story, and having him to talk to was the only reason she'd gotten through it. He hadn't been completely on board, and he thought she was making the biggest mistake of her life, but still, he gave his support.

She shook the thoughts from her mind and went about getting ready for the meeting. No matter what she had done in her past, no matter if it had been a mistake or not, it had all brought her to this point in her life, to this moment when her dreams of a studio in her hometown were about to come true.

There it was. The old, red brick building where Simon Walker Photography had once been located. Vacant for several months since he'd moved his business to Maggie's shop in Hastings.

Shannon couldn't have been more grateful when Maggie suggested she take over the space. At first, she wasn't sure she would be able to afford the rent, and she had said as much to Jamie, who floated the idea of them sharing the space. It was ideal, and everything had fallen into place perfectly. And in minutes, they would walk through the space with the owner, discuss the terms of the lease, and make it official, so they could move in.

The girls climbed out of Jamie's car and stood on the sidewalk in front of the building, waiting for the owner to arrive.

"I can't believe this is happening." Shannon peeked through the window into the empty space.

"Believe it," Jamie replied.

A car drove by and honked, and Shannon startled.

Jamie laughed at her. "You're jumpy."

"I'm just excited. I wish Vern would get here." Shannon's phone went off in her pocket. She didn't recognize the number, but answered it anyway.

"Shannon McGregor Photography."

"Shannon, this is Vernon Howard."

"Hi, Vernon. Jamie and I are here at the building waiting for you."

"That's what I'm calling about."

"Oh? Are you running late?"

"No, I'm calling to let you know I received an offer yesterday to purchase the building outright. I've been thinking of selling for a while now."

"Wait, what? You're selling?"

"Yes, I'm sorry to disappoint you."

"Will the new owner be leasing the space? Can we talk with them?"

"He already has plans for the space, I'm afraid."

Shannon's stomach bottomed out, and she dropped her purse and sank to the sidewalk with her back against the door of the studio that would never be hers.

"I'm so sorry, Shannon. If I hear of any other available spaces, I'll be sure to let you know. Best of luck to you."

And with that, Vernon hung up and left Shannon staring blankly at the street in front of her.

"He sold the building out from under us? What the heck!" Jamie had obviously heard it all and was fuming.

Shannon's heart beat loudly in her ears. The air, which had been warm before, was now stifling, and she began to sweat. She really should've eaten something before she came. The coffee wasn't sitting right.

This couldn't be happening. All her hopes and dreams had been pinned on this studio. Retail space in this area was hard to come by. Impossible, really. And it was gone.

Shannon stood suddenly and began walking.

"Where are you going?" Jamie called after her.

"I need to think."

"Do you want me to come with?"

"No."

"Wait!" Jamie ran over to deliver her purse. "Here."

"Thanks." Shannon turned and walked toward Reeds Lake.

"Call me when it's time to go to Keely's dress fitting and tell me where to pick you up, okay?"

"Okay," she replied weakly.

"It'll be okay, Shannon." Jamie's voice carried after her.

Shannon walked to the end of Wealthy Street and crossed the road to John Collins Park. She sat down on one of the benches and stared out at the morning sun reflecting off the lake. This was not how this day was supposed to go. They should've been walking through the space—their space—and signing papers. Instead it was snatched out from under them.

Her heart was broken.

And the first person she wanted to talk to ... Micah.

Tears sprung to her eyes. Why did she still have to feel such a connection to him after all this time? Why did he have to come back into her life right now? It seemed one thing after another had happened the past few days to bring her down.

Her mind started to form a prayer and then stopped. She hadn't been able to talk to God much in the past ten years. She would start to pray and get angry for all He had taken away from her and stop herself. She couldn't remember the last time she had asked for His help.

The wind blew in off the lake then, causing a hair to tickle her cheek. She inhaled deeply and let it out through her nose. She knew in her mind that God was there for her, that He would never give her more than she could handle, that He wanted what was best for her. But if that was true, why had things taken such a turn ten years ago? Why had her life turned out the way it had?

Breaking up with Micah had been her decision, but she blamed God for allowing the circumstances that had led her there.

Chapter 14

Keely stood on a pedestal in front of three full-length mirrors at her aunt's house. Her mother and Becca stood to her sides while the bridesmaids looked on, all *oohing* and *aahing* over the dress and how beautiful she was, and Shannon and Jamie captured it all. She had always been pretty, but standing there in lace and organza with her delicate Queen Anne neckline added another level to her beauty.

Keely rotated, checking out the open back, before turning to look at the front of the dress again. It fit her hips just right before flowing outward in a mermaid style skirt. "I think it's perfect."

"It's beautiful, honey," her mom gushed.

"You're gorgeous," Becca told her.

The seamstress, Keely's aunt, examined the dress as the bride shifted and turned again. "Looks pretty good if I do say so myself."

Shannon's phone suddenly went off in her pocket. "I'm sorry, Keely. I thought I turned that off."

"You can take it. I don't mind." She was still checking herself out in the mirror.

"Shannon McGregor," she answered.

"Shannon, this is Dr. Ludwig's office calling about your recent test results."

Her heart skipped a beat, and she moved into the hallway for privacy. "Is everything okay?"

"The doctor would like you to come in today if possible to discuss the results. She can squeeze you in around three o'clock if that works for you."

"Um …" Her mind raced, going over the plans for the day. She was supposed to be at the rehearsal by four o'clock. "All right. I can make that work as long as she can see me right at three."

The nurse snickered. "She'll do her best. See you at three."

"Thank you." Her brow broke out with a sheen of sweat, and her heart began racing. What could it be? Had the results shown something awful? She'd had plenty of routine exams and blood work done over the years but had never gotten this kind of call about any of them before.

This is it. Her mind went to all the worst places. *I'm going to die.*

"What's wrong?" Jamie's eyebrows scrunched together with worry. "You look pale."

Shannon shook her head and waved a hand at her. "I'm fine. Still upset about this morning, that's all."

Jamie grumbled. "You and me both."

The ladies started in again with sighs and praises as the veil was placed on Keely's head, and Shannon was reminded that she had a job to do. Her hands shook as she raised her camera. She took a few shots, but they all came out blurry due to her shaking. "Can you take these?" she whispered to Jamie. "I need to get some air."

"Sure thing." Jamie gave her a look of concern as she exited the room.

Shannon walked out of the house to the driveway and placed a phone call. The other end rang and rang, and she thought it might go to voicemail, but Duncan finally answered.

"Hey, I thought I wasn't going to talk to you again until Sunday."

"Can you do something for me?" The tears were burning behind her eyes.

"Anything."

Her chin began to quiver. "Can you pick me up at my apartment and take me to the doctor's office a little before three?"

"Doctor's office? Are you okay?"

"I … I don't know." She fought back tears. "I'm scared, Duncan."

"I'll be there."

Shannon hated this waiting room—the framed black and white photographs of flowers, the pinstriped pattern of the wallpaper, the rack of germ-infested magazines hanging on the wall. She hated that she knew all of the signs posted at the front desk by heart, that there was a snag in the brown carpet by the chair next to the door, and that the receptionist knew her when she walked in.

She stared at the clock on her phone. Five after three. She twiddled her thumbs and stared at the photographs on the wall for the billionth time. Time moved at a snail's pace. Ten after. She wasn't surprised they were running late, but she wished this day would be the exception to the norm. How could she be late for another one of Keely's wedding events? At least she'd managed enough foresight to text Jamie to tell her she might be a little late and ask her to go on ahead to the rehearsal and start taking pictures.

At quarter after, Duncan took her hand in his and kissed the side of her head. "Don't worry."

"I can't help it. What if it's something horrible?" She spoke softly as not to disturb the others waiting.

He squeezed her hand and looked at her with eyes as deep brown as her own. "What if it's not? Maybe it's the opposite. Maybe you're healed!" His expression was hopeful.

She couldn't help but giggle at that and tousled his auburn waves. "If only."

"Miracles can happen."

The office door opened then. "Shannon."

Duncan gave her a quick squeeze. "I'll be right here."

She stood and walked nervously behind the nurse, who took her weight and height and blood pressure and left her in a room alone to wait for Dr. Ludwig. The minutes crawled, and her mind traveled back to the night before her first visit to this office ten years ago.

The stars were brighter than she'd ever seen them before. Maybe it was being out in the country, in the middle of nowhere, parked at Zeb's uncle's farm, with no city lights nearby. Or maybe it was just lying in the back of Micah's truck, snuggled up under the quilt Nana and her sisters had made when she'd graduated high school in June, that made everything seem better. She didn't care. All she cared about was Micah's arms wrapped around her.

"I wish this summer could go on forever." Shannon leaned in and pressed a soft kiss to his lips.

He hummed his appreciation. "Me too." His arms tightened around her as they both gazed up at the night sky.

"Ooh, ooh, shooting star!" Shannon shrieked as one of the twinkly lights above shot across the sky and faded out.

Micah laughed.

"What? Didn't you see it?"

"I saw it."

"Aren't you impressed? I love shooting stars."

"Then you're gonna be really happy tonight."

She propped herself up on her elbow to face him. "Why?"

"There's a meteor shower happening tonight."

"Are you serious?" She lay back next to him again and trained her eyes on the sky, shifting her focus back and forth, searching for another.

"Did you see that one?" Micah suddenly asked.

"Where?"

"To the right."

"I missed it." She pouted.

He rolled onto his side, nuzzling her neck. "You're so cute."

She pushed at him playfully.

"You just keep watching the sky, and I'll watch you." He planted a row of kisses from her ear to her shoulder.

"Micah, you'll miss it."

He pressed his lips to her cheek. "I'm not missing a thing."

She giggled as he started humming the Aerosmith song that had become theirs. "Now who's cute?"

He slid his hand around her back and pulled her closer to him.

She went willingly, wrapping her arm around him.

"I love you," Micah whispered against her lips.

"I love you," she echoed as their mouths came together, sweet and soft and tender.

He rested his forehead against hers. "I don't want to go to Virginia without you."

She rubbed her hand up and down his back. "I know, but it won't be forever."

"A day away from you feels like forever."

Her heart stuttered at his sweet admission.

"Come with me. Move to Virginia. You can study photography anywhere."

"Micah, be serious."

"I'm dead serious."

She sat up and stared down at him. "You want me to move to Virginia? Where am I supposed to live while you're in the dorm?"

"We'll find you an apartment."

"I don't want to live all by myself in a strange town."

"So, go to Liberty."

"I can't afford Liberty, Mr. Full Ride Baseball Scholarship. I can barely afford community college."

"We'll find a way."

"You're so sweet."

Micah sat up and took her face in his hands. "I'm serious. Please think about it."

"I'll think about it."

He kissed the tip of her nose. "Good, because we would have so much fun in Virginia together."

"Oh, you've thought about this, huh?"

"Once we get our degrees, we'll get married and get a place by the ocean—"

"By the ocean? You better get a really good job then."

"I plan on it."

She laughed and lay back again.

"And then we'll start making babies."

"Babies? Plural?"

"Lots of babies." He snuggled up beside her again, his head propped up on one arm, the other draped across her stomach.

"Do I get any say in this?"

"Of course. You can pick a couple of their names."

"You have names picked out already?"

"When we have a boy, I want to name him Matthew after my dad."

Shannon ran her fingertips gently over his arm. Losing his parents at a young age and being the only child had made him want to fill their home with lots of children. And the idea of making those children together made butterflies go crazy in her stomach. "I love that, and I love you so much."

He pressed a soft kiss to her lips. "I mean it. I want to have a family with you. Even if we only have one baby."

"I know. I want a family with you too. I want to give you a great big family, just like mine."

Micah pulled her close. "Our family tree is gonna be HUGE!"

The door opened and brought Shannon back to reality. A middle-aged woman with black hair and streaks of grey stepped into the room. "Hello, Shannon. How are you?"

"Nervous."

"Well, I won't beat around the bush. Your pap smear showed some abnormal cells, and I'd like to do a colposcopy today to see what's going on in there."

"Is it because of my PCOS?"

"There's no reason to believe PCOS would cause you to have abnormal results. Usually, they're unrelated."

"Will it hurt?"

"Not much more than the usual exam. I'll be using a tool that allows me to see inside so I know better what we're dealing with."

Shannon wrung her hands together. "Okay."

"I'll be back with the nurse in a few minutes."

The doctor left a gown for Shannon, who wished in that moment she didn't have to go through all of this alone, that she had someone to hold her hand. She was thankful for Duncan's presence and support—knowing he was in the waiting room calmed her a little—but she wished she'd called her mom. She would've dropped everything to be there. She had been there for every appointment when Shannon was diagnosed with Polycystic Ovary Syndrome. She'd sat at Shannon's bedside eight years ago after her laparoscopic surgery to remove a large cyst from her ovary. What if the doctor found something today? What if she had cancer? Tears welled up in her eyes.

The doctor and nurse returned, and Shannon lay back on the examination table as instructed. Everything was similar to a routine exam at first, then the doctor used a special scope with a camera to get a better look.

"I am seeing some abnormal cells, Shannon."

Shannon started to tremble a little from nerves.

"Nothing to worry about. We can take care of those today with cryotherapy, which is basically freezing them."

"I have a wedding rehearsal I'm photographing today. Will I be able to do that?"

"Yes, you can resume your normal day afterwards. You may experience some mild cramping and discharge, but you should be good to go."

The procedure was uncomfortable, but bearable. Tears slid down the sides of her face, and the nurse gently touched her arm.

"We're almost done, Shannon. You're doing great."

When Dr. Ludwig was through, Shannon released the tension in her body as she let out a breath.

"Well, I see nothing else of concern, Shannon."

More tears burned behind her eyes. "Thank you for making the time for me to come in."

"You're more than welcome. It's best to be safe and get checked out. We'll see you back here for your next appointment."

"Thank you."

While she dressed, she thought about all the times she'd sat in exam rooms at this office, all the bad news she had received here. Thankfully, that wasn't the case on this day, but the fear had been very real. Every time she stepped foot in this place, she assumed the worst. During those times when she had wanted answers, when her periods either wouldn't come or wouldn't stop, this was the place she came. And this was the place where she'd been given the news that would change her life forever—it was highly unlikely that she would be able to conceive a child.

Chapter 15

"Where have you been?" Jamie asked when Shannon finally arrived at the church thirty minutes into rehearsal.

Her camera bag felt heavier than normal on her shoulder, and she was a little queasy from the procedure and from the nerves leading up to the entire appointment. "Something came up. I'll tell you about it later, okay?"

Jamie shrugged. "All right." Her eyes suddenly leapt over Shannon's shoulder, and her grin widened as she maneuvered around Shannon. "Duncan!"

"Hey, you."

Shannon turned in time to see Duncan open his arms and Jamie settle in.

"This town has been boring without you," she told him.

He gave her a tight squeeze before letting go. "You missed me, huh?"

She gave him a hopeful smile. "Didn't you miss me?"

The way he was looking at Jamie made Shannon's eyebrows lift. She'd seen them flirt plenty of times, but there was a seriousness behind his eyes this time. The vibe between them at the moment was one she'd never witnessed before. They seemed happy to see each other, but uncomfortable at the same time. She cleared her throat, which drew Duncan's attention.

He handed Shannon a couple cameras. "Do you have all your stuff?"

She nodded and hugged him. "Thank you. For everything."

"I love you." He kissed her cheek.

"I love you too."

Duncan touched Jamie's arm and gave her a little smile as he walked past her on his way out.

Jamie looked pensive as she watched him go.

"What did I miss?" Shannon asked.

"They've gone over the order of the ceremony and are getting ready to walk through it," Jamie explained as they headed into the main sanctuary.

"I meant between you and my brother." She could've sworn Jamie blushed.

"I don't know what you mean." She tucked a hair behind her ear.

Shannon rolled her eyes. *Yeah, right.*

The members of the bridal party were moving into their places when she and Jamie entered the room. For the hundredth time since Wednesday, her heart took off when she saw Micah. But after their talk last night and after the morning she'd had, her emotions felt like they'd gone haywire. She felt raw and exposed, as if she might burst into tears at any moment.

The music began, and Chase walked across the front of the church behind the pastor and took his place as the bridal party began their processional.

Okay, I can do this.

She willed away the tears. A prayer for renewed strength to get through the weekend was in the forefront of her mind, but she wasn't sure God would hear her after the way she'd given Him the silent treatment all these years. And that made her want to cry even more.

One step at a time, one minute after another, she'd make it through. And then Micah would go back to Virginia with Autumn, and she would try to focus on work and figure out the next step for her business now that the studio wasn't going to happen.

Autumn? *Hmmm.* She scanned the room, wondering if Autumn had shown up yet. There were several young women seated in the pews to the right side of the sanctuary—some she recognized from brunch and the bridal shower as wives or girlfriends of the groomsmen. Maybe one of the others was Autumn.

She went about taking pictures, trying not to dwell on it, and except for a false start because of trouble with the music, the rehearsal was a great success. It was going to be a beautiful wedding.

"Excuse me," a sweet voice with a touch of a Southern accent spoke from behind her shoulder.

Shannon turned to face a lovely, petite girl with strawberry blonde hair and bright blue eyes.

"Hi, I'm Autumn, Micah's friend."

"Oh, Micah's girlfriend, uh ... right. It's good ... nice to meet you," she stammered.

Autumn smiled, which made her even prettier than before. "You're Shannon."

"How did you know?" she asked.

"Micah's told me all about you."

"Oh, okay." Shannon didn't know what to say, and she wondered exactly how much he had told her. Had he told her they'd dated? How she'd broken his heart? Maybe he just told her they were friends.

"Old friends from high school, right?" Autumn asked.

Shannon nodded. "Right. Friends."

"Right." Autumn gave a little grin, which made Shannon think maybe she knew more than she was letting on.

"I see you two have met." Micah strolled up and stood next to Autumn.

"Just," Autumn replied. "I was about to ask Shannon about her cameras." She looked at the camera in Shannon's hand. "I'm in the market for a new one, and I want to invest in a digital SLR, because I love photography, but I have no idea where to start. I was hoping maybe you could point me in the right direction."

"Oh, sure. Maybe we can talk about it after dinner." She held her camera up as she saw Keely and Chase heading her way.

"Of course, don't let me keep you from your job. Photography would be the best job ever. You're sort of my hero."

Autumn was sweet. Shannon liked her already. She wished she didn't. "That's nice of you to say. It's a great job, but a ton of work."

"Maybe you'd let me pick your brain about it later too." She looked giddy.

Her eyes met Micah's for a fraction of a second, then returned to Autumn's. "Sure." Shannon motioned toward the happy couple. "Excuse me."

She walked away quickly, but peeked back over her shoulder at them. They were talking with another couple, standing about a foot apart. They weren't even holding hands. For a couple who had been together for a while, Shannon found that interesting. When she and Micah had been together, they hadn't been able to keep their hands off each other. Butterflies darted about in her stomach at the thought. Even more so when Micah glanced back at her.

Shannon shook her head and walked on. It didn't matter how close they were standing to each other or whether or not they were touching. She was latching on to this tiny detail for no reason. Her heart and mind were a mess ever since he'd walked back into her life. She really had to get over it. He was with Autumn, someone who could probably give him the family she couldn't. Things were as they should be.

Chapter 16

The little white place card on the rehearsal dinner table at Ruth's Chris Steak House bore Micah's name, but it wasn't Autumn's name on the card next to his. Shannon looked up from the seat beside him. Keely's matchmaking ways were obvious in the way she kept pushing the two of them together. He would have to remember to thank her later.

"Hey," he said softly as he took his seat.

"Hi," Shannon replied with camera in hand, shooting pictures of the guests.

Micah watched her press the shutter release then lift her head to scan the room, shifting her lens to the next group of people she was set to capture. He wondered if she ever took a break, because she'd had that camera in front of her pretty face the entire night.

She seemed more relaxed than she had when she'd arrived at the church. Her eyes had been rimmed in red, as if she'd been crying, and it ate away at him, the wondering why. Was she upset about their talk last night? Maybe he shouldn't have gotten so close, but he was still so drawn to her. He hadn't been able to help himself.

Shannon glanced over at him then across the table at Autumn before she stood and went to work taking pictures again. It felt strange and awkward having the two of them meet. Not that Autumn didn't know everything there was to know about his relationship with Shannon—after he found out she was the wedding photographer, he'd filled Autumn in on their whole story—but Shannon didn't know the truth about Autumn, and that felt like a lie by omission.

His thoughts remained consumed by Shannon, so much that he jumped when Autumn reached across the table and touched his arm.

"Gee, I didn't mean to scare you. Are you all right?"

"Fine."

She scrunched her lips to the side in disapproval. "You forget that I know you, Micah Shaw. Ten years of friendship have taught me what that face means."

He smirked at her. "This face?"

"I know when you're in deep thought mode." She paused and narrowed her eyes at him. "Are you going to tell her about us?" she whispered.

He blew out a breath. "What difference would it make now?"

"Maybe all the difference in the world."

"I don't know. This doesn't only affect me."

"Don't worry about me for a minute. I did all of this for you, remember." She squeezed his arm. "You should tell her. Tonight."

"Are you sure?"

"Absolutely."

He took her hand and kissed her knuckles. "You're so good to me."

Her smile lit up her face. "What are friends for?" She turned away to chat with Keely's sister then.

Micah's mind raced. He'd had no intention of telling Shannon the true nature of his relationship with Autumn. Up until now, the reasons they were together had been kept between the two of them. They hadn't let another soul in on it. But Autumn had basically given him permission to tell, and he wanted Shannon to know the truth. He wondered if it *would* make a difference to her. He doubted it, but how would he know unless he tried?

He watched Shannon move about the room with camera in hand. He'd tell her. Tonight. And if she didn't care, then life would remain the way it had been and nothing would be lost. But if he kept it to himself, nothing could possibly be gained.

When the appetizers arrived, Shannon and Jamie took their seats at the table, and Micah was happy to see Shannon set her equipment down. She looked tired.

Dinner was delicious—prime rib, melt-in-your-mouth garlic mashed potatoes, tasty creamed spinach, and a decadent chocolate cake for dessert. Micah couldn't help noticing that Shannon ate chicken instead of steak, some of the spinach, but none of her potatoes or cake. He remembered all of the greens in her refrigerator and wondered why on earth, with the slender figure she'd always had, did she need to watch what she ate.

There was so much about her he didn't know, didn't understand. Like why she was on birth control. That one still ate away at him. But was any of it really his business? No, it wasn't. Still, he couldn't help but want to know everything, every detail about her life, about who she was now, who she'd been for the past ten years.

He pierced into the cake and lifted a piece on his fork in Shannon's direction. "Want a bite?"

She seemed taken aback and glanced nervously across the table at Autumn.

Right. Autumn. My girlfriend.

"I'm fine, thanks."

He gave a weak grin in response.

"So, what's your favorite thing about being a wedding photographer?" Autumn asked Shannon.

Shannon got a dreamy look in her eyes. "The people. Hands down. I love watching them, getting to know them through my lens, catching the connections and interactions without them even knowing I'm doing it. Absolute favorite thing."

"That sounds wonderful, and you're so good at it."

"Oh, have you seen my pictures?" Shannon asked.

Autumn nodded enthusiastically. "Micah showed me your website. People are probably lining up for you to photograph their weddings. Your work is stunning."

Micah watched Shannon and saw a hint of a blush color her cheeks. *She* was stunning.

"Thank you, Autumn. That's sweet. I've worked really hard to get where I am today."

"And I hear you're opening a studio of your own. That's amazing."

"I ..." Shannon pressed her lips together.

Micah's heart ached at the tears pooling in Shannon's eyes. "What's wrong?" He touched her knee under the table.

She pushed her chair out and stood. "I have to ... I'm sorry ... excuse me." Her dark, silky hair swished back and forth as she walked swiftly away from their table.

"Oh, no, did I say something wrong?" Autumn asked.

Micah looked over at Jamie, who was seated to Shannon's other side. "Is she okay?"

Jamie shook her head. "The studio fell through today. Owner sold the building right out from under us."

"No."

"Yes. The jerk."

Micah turned to Autumn. "I'll be right back."

Autumn smiled knowingly.

He moved as quickly as he could into the lobby of the restaurant. Shannon stood by the window, staring out at the street, wiping at her cheeks. Instinct told him to take her in his arms, but he wasn't sure he should do that right now.

"Hey." He walked slowly toward her.

She wiped faster at her cheeks, as if that would hide her tears.

"Jamie told me about the studio. I'm so sorry, Shannon."

She took a deep breath, but hiccuped instead.

Micah stepped closer, leaving his arms at his sides, palms open toward her to make it known that he was there if she needed a hug.

She took advantage of the invitation and stepped into him, resting her head against his chest, gripping the lapels of his suit jacket.

He slid his hands up her arms and rested them around her upper back, holding her to him, and it felt so right.

"Why do all these bad things keep happening to me?" she whimpered. "I thought this was it. At least one of my dreams was going to come true."

He wondered what bad things she meant. "*One* of your dreams?"

She didn't respond to that. "We were so close. I could picture our logos in that front window. I imagined all the people we would meet because of that space. It's in such a great location. It was perfect. Why didn't it happen, Micah? Why does nothing ever work out how I think it's going to?"

"I don't know." He wrapped his arms tighter around her and held her while she let out all her tears. "But most of the time when things don't work out, it's because something better is about to come along."

She was quiet for a minute. "You mean like you and Autumn?"

"Me and Autumn?" he asked.

She nodded against his chest. "Yeah, like how you thought Jacqueline was the one for you and that didn't work out, but then you found Autumn."

Micah didn't know what to say to that. He hadn't been thinking of Jacquie or Autumn at all.

"She's lovely, Micah." She sniffled as she looked up at him. "I mean it. You couldn't have found a better girl."

"You barely know her. She could be a stalker like Jacquie." He winked at her.

"She's special. I can tell." She lifted her hands from his chest, and he reluctantly let go.

Looking down into her eyes, he wiped away a streak of tears from her cheek. "So are you."

She turned her gaze to the window again.

"Why were you late tonight? I thought I saw Duncan."

"You did. He brought me. I had a ... something came up."

Yet another subject skirted. What was she hiding from him?

"Would you mind if I drove you home tonight?" he asked.

Her eyes found his again. "Jamie's taking me home."

"Can I take you ... so we can talk? There's something I really need to say."

She motioned toward the dining room. "What about Autumn?"

A loud, deafening siren suddenly sounded, startling them both. People began funneling from the restaurant out into the street.

"What's happening?" Micah asked Chase when he and Keely came rushing toward them.

"Fire alarm," Chase replied.

They followed along with the crowd until they were safely gathered across the street. The air was cool on this cloudy June evening, and Micah noticed both Shannon and Autumn shiver at the breeze. He was torn as to whom he should give his jacket to. He peeled it off and held it out to Autumn.

She shook her head. "Shannon looks chilly. Let her wear it." She spoke loud enough to be heard and nudged him in her direction.

He smirked at her. She and Keely should start a matchmaking service together. "Here." He laid his jacket over Shannon's shoulders.

"Thanks."

That lovely blush was back in her cheeks. He itched to caress one.

The restaurant patrons stood on the sidewalk as the police and fire truck arrived. They entered the building and emerged soon after. One of the officers stepped up to the group and addressed them. "False alarm, folks. The building is safe to enter. If any of you knows the identity of the person who pulled the fire alarm, we would appreciate your assistance."

Micah followed behind Shannon, watching her walk, wishing he could turn off these feelings he had for her.

She handed him his jacket and took her seat, and he sat down beside her again. His fork was still sitting in the same spot he had left it with one sliver of cake sitting atop it. He was about to offer it to Shannon when he noticed her face go pale as a ghost, her eyes shifting back and forth frantically.

"What's wrong?"

"My camera's gone."

"Are you sure?" he asked.

She crouched down and looked under the table and around her chair. "Yes, I left everything here. My cameras, my bag. It's all gone."

Jamie returned to the table then.

"Jamie, did you take my equipment when you went outside?" There was an edge of panic to Shannon's voice.

"No, I left it here."

She pulled her own chair out and gasped. "What the heck? My stuff is gone."

"Mine's gone too." The tears were back in Shannon's eyes again.

"Come on," Jamie said. "We need to report this to those cops outside before they leave."

Shannon let out an exasperated breath as she stood. "What is with this day? Seriously? It's one thing after another."

Micah watched the girls leave the banquet room. He wished he could help. Having things stolen was a terrible feeling, a violation. He'd had it happen in Virginia once. Someone had broken into his apartment and taken all his electronics. Nothing important—just stuff—but it was enough to take away the feeling of security that he'd always felt living where he had. He was sure that's how the girls were feeling now—unsafe—and he hated that. He wanted to make everything right for Shannon. She seemed to be having a very rough day, and all he wanted was to make it better.

He headed out to see if they'd found a police officer, and as he entered the main dining room, he spotted a woman seated alone at a small table. She ducked behind a menu, but he knew who it was before he even approached her.

Jacqueline.

Chapter 17

"I can't believe this is happening after the day I've already have." Shannon plopped down on the curb outside, not giving a thought to the dress she was wearing or the dirt and grease she was probably sitting on. "How are we supposed to shoot the weddings tomorrow with no cameras?"

"I have a backup camera, a couple lenses, and a flash that I can make work if I don't find anything else. Maybe one of the local camera shops would rent us some equipment," Jamie suggested.

"I need mine by nine o'clock, and I don't think many open before then on a Saturday."

"I'm going to make some calls, see if anyone can help us. Don't worry, Shan." Jamie squeezed her forearm. "We're going to figure this out."

She took a deep breath in. It felt like she'd been doing that all day, trying to catch her breath from blow after blow. A nauseous sensation came over her, thinking about someone stealing her equipment— especially the memory cards filled with all the pictures from the day. All those moments lost. She could feel her dinner threatening to come back up as she stood. This felt like more than a nervous stomach, though, and she suddenly wondered if it was something she ate. "I think I might be sick."

Jamie stood up after her with phone in hand. "Oh, no."

Shannon looked over just in time to see the color leave Jamie's face as she covered her mouth and took off across the street for the nearest garbage can, barely making it in time. Shannon followed after her friend. "Jame, are you okay?"

Jamie spit into the can. "Gross. I hate throwing up."

Shannon couldn't help but laugh. "Does anyone like throwing up?"

"You know what I mean. Blah. I need some water. My mouth tastes disgusting."

"I hope you're not so sick you can't shoot that wedding tomorrow."

Jamie shook her head. "No, I think it was a combination of eating too much, being upset about our equipment, and standing up too fast."

"Are you sure?"

"Yeah, I'm gonna go get a drink and make some calls. I'll let you know what I find out."

Shannon still felt queasy. She wondered if any other guests were experiencing what they were. After the day she'd had, it wouldn't surprise her at all to add food poisoning to the list.

As she wandered back across the street to the restaurant, her mind returned to the camera situation, and she tried to formulate a solution to her problem. She pulled out her phone and opened the Facebook app, posting a brief message on her personal page, asking if anyone out there had any camera equipment she could borrow for tomorrow. It was a desperate plea, but maybe someone had an extra camera or lens or flash she could borrow.

It felt like this day was conspiring against her. She checked the time on her phone and noticed the date read "Friday, June 10." She was suddenly floored. June tenth? Of course it was. The tenth of June was the anniversary of her first official date with Micah back in 2000.

Unbelievable.

"I don't know what you're talking about!" a woman's high-pitched voice cried. "Micah, stop!"

Shannon turned to see Micah ushering Jacqueline from the restaurant by the arm.

"Are the cops still here?" Micah asked.

"No." Shannon shifted her attention to Jacqueline. "*You're* still here?"

"Of course, I am," Jacqueline replied. "We still have things to talk about."

"Where are the cameras?" Micah snapped.

Shannon's mouth fell open. "You took our cameras?"

Jacqueline wiggled her arm from Micah's grasp. "No, I did *not* take your cameras."

"I don't believe you." Micah glared at her. "It's a little too convenient. You being here, the fire alarm being pulled, and Shannon's equipment going missing."

"I would never do such a thing. You know me better than that."

Micah shook his head. "I don't think I ever knew you or what you were capable of."

The distress on Jacqueline's face was plain as day. "You know me better than anyone."

"Well, then that's sad if you have nobody else."

"So, what about my cameras then?" Shannon asked.

"I might know something, but I didn't take them."

"What do you mean?"

Jacqueline acted coy, and Micah stepped toward her with impatience in his eyes. "Jacquie, what?"

"I saw who pulled the fire alarm."

"Who was it?" Shannon asked.

Jacqueline's eyes fixed on Micah. "The only way I'll tell you is if I can have some time with you to talk. I feel like you aren't giving me a chance."

Micah's annoyance was obvious, and he looked at Shannon as if to ask what he should do.

Shannon pleaded with her eyes. If Jacqueline could give them something to go on, maybe the police would have a better chance of retrieving their equipment. After all, every one of the pictures from Keely's dress fitting and rehearsal were on the memory cards in those bags.

"Fine." Micah gave in. "I'm going to give Shannon a ride home first."

"Oh, no you don't," Jacquie declared. "You aren't leaving my sight the rest of the night."

Micah swallowed hard and gritted his teeth.

"I can get a ride with Jamie, Micah." A stab of disappointment hit Shannon then, wondering what he needed to tell her. "I'll see you tomorrow."

He left Jacqueline's side and took Shannon's arm, walking them far enough away that the freaky ex couldn't hear their conversation.

"I'll get the truth out of her. I promise."

She squeezed his hand. "I know you will. In the meantime, I have to find some equipment to shoot with tomorrow morning, so I better get busy with that."

Micah suddenly leaned forward and pressed a kiss to her forehead. "I'm sorry you've had a bad day."

"A really bad day." She managed a weak smile.

"Tomorrow is fresh ..." He grinned at her.

"With no mistakes in it." She finished the sentence, a quote from *Anne of Green Gables* that Nana had used often over the years. Just the fact that he remembered warmed her heart.

Chapter 18

Whatever that loud banging noise was, Shannon wished it would go away. She preferred to stay in her happy little dream world, snuggled up in Micah's arms, lying on a blanket in the grass at Aunt Pauline's, listening to the sounds of summer. Her eyelids lifted slowly, heavy from all her worry over how she was possibly going to shoot a wedding with no equipment. A couple people had offered her a lens or two, but most area photographers had weddings of their own, which they needed most or all of their equipment for. She couldn't blame them for not helping her. If they could've, she knew they would've.

A knocking sound had her sitting up in bed. Who was knocking at seven o'clock in the morning? Was it at the neighbor's apartment? It grew quickly from a knock to a steady pounding, and she jumped from bed and raced to the door. Maybe it was Jamie. Maybe she'd found some equipment. Who else would be at her door at this hour?

She released the lock, praying a solution to her problem was on the other side of the door. But it wasn't Jamie she found there. Instead, Simon Walker breezed past her into the apartment, dressed in a dark grey suit with his nut brown hair styled neatly, carrying a box.

"Simon? What are you doing here?"

"We come bearing gifts." His wife, Maggie, was on his tail, also dressed nicely, carrying a camera bag over her shoulder. "Heard you needed some equipment."

Simon set the box on the dining table, and Shannon's eyes nearly popped out of her head as he unloaded a couple Canon cameras and began attaching flashes to them.

Maggie placed the camera bag next to the box and unzipped it, revealing a variety of lenses. She pushed a section of sandy blonde hair away from her face. "We brought a few fixed lenses—a 28mm, a 50, 85, 100mm macro. There's even a 28-300 L series in here for ya. And there are enough memory cards to cover two weddings."

"Where did all this come from?" she asked.

"We had a few we weren't using today, and the others came from photographer friends of ours."

She hoped after all the tears shed yesterday that she wouldn't end up crying again today, but tears sprung to her eyes, and she covered her face with her hands and let them come, the stress and worry dissolving away.

"Thank you," she mumbled into her hands.

Maggie's arms wrapped around her. "We've got your back, girl. We always will."

Shannon moved from Maggie into the kitchen and grabbed a tissue, wiping away the tears. "I don't know what to say or how to thank you."

"Just pay it forward someday." Simon leaned back against her kitchen counter.

"You know we would've done anything to help you." Maggie moved next to her husband, his arm wrapping around her lower back and resting on her waist.

They were so sweet together, and Shannon's heart ached for Micah. She turned away before she started crying again and began looking through the equipment, cataloguing what she had to work with.

"How did the meeting with Vern go?"

Shannon winced at the question.

"That bad?" His brow furrowed. "I thought it was a done deal."

She looked at him sadly. "He sold the building."

"No way."

"Yep."

"Maybe you can rent it from the new owner," he suggested.

"He already has plans for the space."

Simon's shoulders sank. "I'm so sorry, Shannon. That's not cool."

A sigh escaped her. "It's his building. He had to make the right choice for him, I guess. Even if it wasn't how I thought things were gonna go."

"I'm very familiar with that feeling," Maggie told her. "If things had gone the way I'd planned, my life would look very different right now." She turned into Simon and wrapped her arms around his waist. "But God had something better for me."

Shannon smiled, knowing what Maggie had been through with a broken engagement years ago.

"God's got something amazing planned for you, Shannon. I believe that."

She wasn't so sure, and that must've shown in her expression.

"You do know that, right?"

Shannon shrugged, not making eye contact.

Maggie walked over and put an arm around her. "When I was at a low point and my life seemed to be falling apart, when I didn't believe God was listening to me, my family reminded me that God sees the big picture when we can't. He knows the plans He has for us, and He wants our happiness. He really does."

The tears burned behind Shannon's eyes again. Deep down, she believed that. But if God knew having a family with Micah would make her happy, why would He take away her ability to have children? She didn't understand.

"But He wants us to rely on Him to find that happiness," Maggie continued. "In His time, not ours. It may not seem like it now, when things aren't going how you want them to, but all things work together for good to those that love God. Don't forget that."

With Maggie's words and her quote of a beloved verse in the book of Romans, something in Shannon clicked. She hadn't been relying on God at all. She'd been closed off to Him for a very long time—from the moment she found out she couldn't have kids, really. She hadn't trusted that God was working things out for her. She'd only seen the things that were taken away from her. What might she have missed out on while she'd been trying to find happiness on her own?

"We'll keep our eyes and ears open and pray," Maggie told her. "There's a better studio space out there for you, and God's going to help us find it."

Shannon forced the tears back, put her arm around Maggie, and gave her a side hug. "You guys are the best."

"Well, you're important to us," Maggie said with a smile.

"And we have to stick together," Simon stated.

"Yes, we do." Her phone chimed from her bedroom alerting her of a text. "Excuse me for a second."

A text from Jamie read "Did you get equipment?"

"I did!" Shannon replied.

"So relieved. I got some too. Any news from Micah on our stuff?"

"Not yet."

"I'll be there to take you to the church a little before nine."

"See you then."

Shannon returned to the kitchen. "Jamie got some equipment too."

"Yeah, she just texted to let us know." Maggie held up her phone.

Shannon was thankful for the great community of photographers they were a part of. The people she'd come to know because of their quarterly photographer gatherings had changed her life. They'd helped guide her as she built her business, given advice, referred clients to her for events and weddings. And this morning had reminded her what an amazing source of support and encouragement they all were. Not to mention, three of the biggest blessings in her life had come from that group—Maggie, Simon, and Jamie.

Shannon felt a peace she hadn't felt in a long time after her conversation with Maggie. She still didn't know what God was doing or how things were going to turn out, but she had a renewed confidence that there was a plan and He was going to reveal it to her. She just needed to do her best to be patient and accept whatever came.

Despite her newfound peace, she started to feel a little on edge as Jamie drove her to the church, wondering how Micah's conversation with Jacqueline had gone. Was no message from him a good thing or a bad thing? Did he find out what she knew? Or was it a dead end and that's why he hadn't called or texted?

Micah was standing outside, talking on his phone when they arrived.

"I want to hear everything." Jamie pulled up in front of the building. "Call me tonight if it's not too late."

"I'm sure I'll be wiped out by then. Why don't you come to my parents' house for lunch tomorrow. One o'clock."

"Okay." She looked excited, probably at the prospect of seeing Duncan. "How are you getting home tonight?"

"Duncan's dropping his car off at the reception for me."

"All right. Have a great wedding."

"You too." Shannon waved as Jamie drove off, then hesitantly approached Micah, not wanting to interrupt his conversation, but anxious to know if he'd learned anything.

"I have to go," he told whoever he'd been talking to.

"Anything from Jacqueline?" she asked.

"I'm taking care of it." He looked serious.

"What does that mean?"

"I don't want you to worry about it today, okay. Just focus on the wedding." His eyes stopped on the equipment over her shoulders. "Hey, you got equipment!"

"Some really great friends hooked me up."

The happiness showed on his face. "That's amazing."

She headed toward the church doors, and he walked quickly to get ahead of her and hold the door. "Why are *you* here so early? Hair and makeup?" she teased.

He smirked. "Chase wanted me to deliver a gift to his bride before all the momentum of the day picks up."

"That's so nice."

"Yeah, he's sweet that way."

She stopped when she realized he wasn't walking into the church with her and turned to look at him.

"I have to get back to Chase." He pointed over his shoulder toward the parking lot.

"Oh, right." She let out a nervous laugh and walked swiftly toward the room where the girls were getting ready.

"Shannon!" Micah's voice carried down the hallway behind her.

She rotated to face him as he caught up to her, moved her camera equipment from her shoulders to the floor, and pulled her into an embrace.

"What's this for?" she asked, feeling quite content to stay put for a while.

"I wanted to start your day on a happy note."

She giggled softly into his shoulder. "That's sweet, Micah. It's already been a good morning, and you just made it better."

"Good. I'm glad. I hated seeing you have such a hard time yesterday."

"It's not up to you to make my day happy."

He let go of her then. "I know, but I still want to." He gave her that cute little closed mouth smile that had always melted her heart, gave her back her equipment, and slowly walked away down the hall.

Shannon watched his every step, wondering if he'd turn back to look at her. Just as he reached the door, he glanced back with another sweet smile and nervously ran his hand over the back of his neck as he walked out.

She sighed. *If only things were different.*

The sound of chattering girls led her down the hallway to Keely and her bridesmaids. Two hair stylists and a makeup artist were there to work on the girls' wedding looks, and Shannon captured it all—the sweet compliments to each other, the laughter, the inside jokes they all shared. This little group seemed more like sisters than friends, and it made Shannon miss Sophia.

She missed their high school days—sitting up late, pigging out on pizza, talking about boys, laughing until their stomachs hurt. Only a year after her PCOS diagnosis, Sophia had graduated and left for New York. She hadn't been there when they discovered Shannon had a cyst. She hadn't come home for Shannon's procedure. When she did come home, it was usually for a quick weekend visit, and she spent most of the time on her phone, wrapped up in her own little world. Things weren't the same between them, which saddened her.

She shook off thoughts of her sister and went back to work.

"Do you think I should open it now?" Keely asked of the small square package Micah had delivered to her for Chase.

"Heck, yeah," Becca replied. "He wanted you to have it this morning. Maybe it's something for you to wear for the wedding."

Keely opened the envelope Chase had sent with the gift. She read it over, then sighed and read it aloud. "Keely, you are priceless to me. More precious than diamonds. I love you. Chase."

The girls all sighed or *aww'd*.

She tore off the wrapping paper and opened the box to find a delicate diamond bracelet within along with a little note that read "Something to wear down the aisle."

"See! I told you!" Becca declared.

Keely touched it lovingly. "He's the sweetest."

"And he'll be your husband in about four hours," one of the bridesmaids said.

Keely squealed, which elicited the same from the rest of the girls, and they all met up in a group hug.

Shannon was so thankful for the equipment that had been lent to her, which allowed her to capture this precious moment.

When the guys arrived at the church, Shannon snuck away for a bit to photograph them getting ready. Groomsmen were usually much lower maintenance than the girls were, so it never took long to snap pictures of them helping each other with their ties and such.

But when Shannon walked in, there was a hush over the room she hadn't expected. The mood felt somber. Most of the guys were already dressed and sitting quietly, staring at their phones. Micah and Chase were speaking quietly at the far end of the room. Keely's dad was red in the face, and Chase's dad was nowhere to be found.

Micah spotted her near the door.

"Did I come at a bad time?" She spoke in a whisper as he approached, but it was so quiet in there that it sounded like she had spoken at full volume.

He gently took her arm and led her into the hallway.

"What is it? What's happening?"

"It was Georgia, Chase's mom."

"What was Georgia?"

"Jacqueline told me that a woman in a blue dress pulled the fire alarm last night. A woman that was with our party at the rehearsal dinner." He pressed his lips together and shook his head. "I asked some of the bridesmaids. Georgia was the only woman wearing a blue dress."

Shannon's mouth fell open. "You're sure?"

"I showed Jacquie a picture of Georgia, and she confirmed she was the one."

"Why would she do that?"

"Apparently, she does not approve of Keely."

Shannon was floored. "Are you serious? Keely is the sweetest girl on the planet."

"Yes, but she's from the wrong family. Georgia had plans for Chase to marry into another well-to-do family to merge together two very successful business empires. She tried to get him to break things off with Keely last year and marry this other girl. Chase would have none of it. This was her way of trying to sabotage the wedding."

The thought sickened her. And then she had another. "What about our cameras?"

"Georgia."

Shannon's mouth fell open.

"I went back to the restaurant today, and a couple guys admitted she paid them to take your stuff and toss it in the dumpster out back."

Shannon backed against the wall behind her, completely shocked and appalled. "Who does that?"

"A woman with messed up priorities."

"She seemed ... normal."

"Not everyone is as they seem."

Shannon gasped. "Keely doesn't know, does she?"

Micah shook his head. "Chase is trying to decide how to tell her or if he should wait until after the ceremony."

"She'll be heartbroken."

"I think he should tell her now. Something this big ... she should have the right to decide if she wants to go through with it."

Her heart leapt into her throat. Even though Micah had no idea, what he'd said could've easily applied to them as well. She had made a huge decision for the two of them—leaving him because of her diagnosis, so he'd have a chance at a family with someone else someday.

Over the years, there were plenty of times when she'd doubted herself, wondering what might've happened if she'd told him the truth and let him decide. Hearing him say those words now, even if they weren't about their relationship, touched on that insecurity and brought it all to the surface.

She breathed deeply and set her camera on a nearby table. "So ... I guess we'll probably never get our stuff back. All those pictures of Keely's dress fitting and the rehearsal are lost."

"Actually, the guys didn't toss it."

"They probably sold it or something, right?"

"No, they put it in a storage closet there at the restaurant. The whole thing kind of creeped them out."

"Not enough to say no to taking the money, though, right?"

"Well, yeah, there's that." He shrugged his shoulders. "But your equipment is in the trunk of the Lexus."

"What? Micah! Are you serious?"

He nodded.

Shannon threw her arms around his neck. "Thank you! Thank you! Thank you!"

He laughed and wrapped his arms around her.

Relief engulfed her. She loosened her hold on him and spontaneously pressed her lips against his.

His entire body stiffened.

She stepped away, astonished at herself. "I'm ... I didn't mean to—"

In a millisecond, his fingers threaded through her hair, and his lips were on hers.

Her knees went weak as warmth spread through her entire body. Micah was kissing her. It felt so familiar, so right. She slid her arms around his neck, slowly this time, slipping her fingers through his soft, blond hair, kissing him back with all the passion she'd buried. His arms wound around her, locking her securely against him, as his lips moved with hers, stirring a deep yearning within her she thought she'd never feel again. Oh, how she'd missed this. Him. It felt like no time had passed at all, their kisses transporting them back to happier times.

Lips slowed, foreheads touched, breaths mingled.

"Shannon." His voice was deep and thick and sweet. "I've wanted to do that since I picked you up on the side of the road."

"So have I," she whispered.

"You have no idea how much I've missed you."

"I've missed you too."

His thumbs softly brushed her cheeks.

She wanted to kiss him again, but her situation hadn't changed. She still had traitorous ovaries. And as good as they were together, this one very important detail she'd kept from him could break them apart forever. But, like Keely, didn't he have the right to know everything? More and more, she felt like he did.

And then she remembered Autumn.

She stepped out of his arms and straightened her back. "We shouldn't have done that. Your poor girlfriend. I feel awful right now."

"You need to know something about me and Autumn. We're not—"

Chase swept out of the room and past them just then. "I'm telling her," he declared. "Wish me luck."

Shannon lowered her head. Her heart ached for Keely. "What a nightmare."

"You haven't seen them together much." Micah watched his friend walk to the opposite end of the hallway where the girls were. "They were meant for each other. They really were. And I know they'll get through this. Even if they don't get married today."

"You think they'll postpone?"

He shrugged his shoulders. "I guess that will be up to Keely." Micah's phone rang, and he glanced at it. "I have to take this. Please don't go far. I want to talk more."

Shannon nodded as he walked toward the exit. She grabbed her camera and wandered down the hallway toward the girls' room as Chase and Keely walked out, her hand in his. Keely looked over at her with trepidation, and Shannon wished she could give her a hug to instill a little strength in her before Chase broke the news.

It was a while before the door opened again, and Keely walked out with red eyes and blotchy cheeks. Her perfect makeup was no longer perfect. Her happy eyes and joyful smile had been erased.

Keely reached her hand out to Shannon and led her back into the girls' room with her.

Shannon watched Chase walk away sadly and meet up with Micah, before she closed the door behind them.

"What's wrong?" Becca asked her sister.

Keely started to get choked up again and brushed away a fat tear that slipped down her cheek. "Chase's mom tried to sabotage the wedding," she mumbled.

Gasps filled the room.

"No way."

"Why would she do that?"

"What did she do?"

"She pulled the alarm at the restaurant, and she actually paid someone to steal Shannon's equipment and throw it in a dumpster."

"No!"

"Are you serious?"

The girls were all flabbergasted.

"When we got home from that disaster of a rehearsal dinner last night, we found the box with my grandparents' dishes from the 1940s—the dishes Grandma gave us for our wedding gift—on the floor, most of them broken. We thought it had fallen accidentally, but now I'm not so sure. If she's capable of all this, I wouldn't put it past her to destroy our dishes too."

Shannon felt sick to her stomach hearing that. Would Georgia be that blatantly cruel? She *had* made a comment about having fine china at the bridal shower. The vintage dishes must not have been good enough for her.

"I just ..." Keely started to cry again. "She was never anything but kind to me, but I guess that was all an act. All these years, she resented me for taking Chase away from some debutante he was supposed to marry so their families' businesses could merge into some gigantic multi-billion dollar company."

Some of the girls moved closer and put their arms around her.

"How am I supposed to go through with this now? How can I marry into that family?"

"What does Chase say?" Shannon asked.

"He wants to marry me." A little smile broke through her sadness. "He doesn't care about his family's money. He's willing to walk away from all of it for me. But can I really ask him to do that?"

"What did you tell him?"

"That I needed to think and talk to my girls." She wiped away tears again. "I love him, you guys. I can't imagine my life without him in it."

Shannon's heart ached, remembering her kiss with Micah in the hallway. She'd lived years of her life without him in it, and she knew a thing or two about regrets. If Keely didn't marry Chase, it would be the one decision she'd wish she could take back.

"Then marry him," Shannon blurted. "Forget his mother, forget the fortune he's giving up. Marry the man you love. It can be that simple. Just choose love. Choose Chase."

"I want to." Keely started smiling, which quickly turned into happy laughter. "I'm gonna do it."

The girls all hugged her, then Keely moved closer to Shannon and squeezed her tightly. "Thank you."

Shannon smiled. "You're welcome. You won't regret it."

Keely looked her in the eyes then and whispered, "Choose love, Shannon. Choose Micah." She winked and headed for the door with the girls following, leaving Shannon behind with her words.

Shannon recalled Maggie's words from that morning, reminding her that God sees the big picture and there is a greater plan. Could Micah be part of that plan? Is that why he came back into her life after all this time? The fact still remained that she couldn't have kids. Could she make Micah happy without them? Would he be content with her alone?

The girls' giggles drew Shannon in, and she joined them in the hallway outside the room. Keely's steps quickened on her way to Chase, who was pacing at the opposite end of the hallway.

"I want to marry you, Chase Pennington!" Keely cried.

His face lit up, and he moved toward her in three long strides.

Shannon raised her camera in time to capture him meeting her in a kiss, lifting her off of the floor, and spinning her around.

The girls clapped and cheered as did the guys from their doorway. Shannon's eyes locked with Micah's as they both clapped.

Shannon wanted to choose love. She wanted to choose Micah. But if she told him the truth, would he choose her?

Chapter 19

The sweet sounds of a piano and violin duet playing "God Gave Me You" floated softly into the foyer as guests wandered into the church, stopping to sign the guest book before being seated.

Micah stared out the window, unable to stop thinking about Shannon. Especially after that unexpected, amazing, heart racing, blood pumping, never-want-it-to-end kiss. He could've stood there in the hallway kissing her all day. Forget about the wedding. Forget about Chase's awful mother. Forget about crazy Jacqueline. Her lips on his, that was all he needed in life.

Autumn scurried across the parking lot ten minutes before the wedding. Her strawberry blonde hair was curled neatly, half pinned up atop her head. Her cheeks were rosy, lips pink to match the flowers on her dress.

"Hi." Her face lit up when she saw him. "Sorry I'm so late."

He hugged her and kissed her cheek. "You look beautiful."

"Thank you." She gave him a once over. "You're not so bad yourself."

He straightened the jacket of his tux and struck a pose, and she let out a little laugh.

The foyer had mostly cleared out, except for family or guests like her, arriving at the last minute. Her eyes scanned the room. "What a weird day, huh?"

"You can say that again. I'm just glad they're going through with it."

"So am I. They're so great together." She leaned closer and spoke in a whisper. "What his mom did was horrible."

"I know. She left on a plane today."

Autumn's eyes widened. "Wow!"

"His dad stayed, at least."

"Oh, really, he's here?"

"Yeah. He loves Chase, and he doesn't want Keely to feel alienated from the family because of this."

"I hope it all works out."

"I'm sure things won't be pretty when he gets home."

Autumn giggled. "I think not."

Micah's eyes caught on Shannon as she moved into position to photograph the grandparents being seated, and his heart rate kicked up a notch. All of his attention focused on her, and he hadn't realized Autumn was talking until she touched his arm.

He startled. "Huh?"

"That's my cue."

"Sorry, what?"

She nodded toward Shannon and the white-haired couple entering through the sanctuary doors then pointed to the side door. "I'm gonna sneak in and find a seat."

He touched her arm. "See you after."

She smiled sweetly and left him where he stood, ashamed for tuning her out the way he had. He couldn't help it. When Shannon was in a room, she was all he saw.

The bridesmaids came into the foyer then and began lining up to enter the sanctuary. Becca wound her arm through Micah's and led him into position.

He couldn't drag his eyes away from Shannon, standing in the aisle to photograph each bridal party couple as they entered. He was sure to give her his cutest grin when he passed by. She didn't respond at all aside from pressing the shutter on her camera. She was completely focused on her job—a real pro.

At the front of the aisle, Chase was the picture of cool, calm, and collected—like he'd been ready for this his entire life. And when the doors opened to reveal Keely in her wedding dress, Micah looked over at his friend, who had tears in his eyes and the biggest smile he'd ever worn. It was enough to get Micah all choked up. This was a huge day for his best friend. He was marrying the love of his life, and Micah couldn't have been happier for him. For them.

He noticed Shannon crouched down at the front of the aisle, capturing Keely's processional. She rotated and snapped a few photos of Chase's reaction to his bride, then looked over the top of her camera at Micah. For the briefest of moments, her lips curved up. Then she stood and snapped more pictures of Keely before moving back the aisle and capturing the entire bridal party on the stage.

Once again, Micah was in awe of her.

The ceremony began and, despite wanting to keep his eyes on Shannon, he had to pay attention so he would remember to give Chase the ring at the appropriate time. He'd never been the best man in a wedding before, and he didn't want to blow it.

When Becca stepped up to the microphone to recite scripture, Micah's eyes turned to the audience, and he found Autumn halfway back to his left.

"Love is patient, love is kind. It does not envy. It does not boast."

When he thought about Autumn, he felt comfort, friendship, companionship. She was definitely all the things the verses in I Corinthians described.

"It is not self-seeking. It is not easily angered. It keeps no record of wrongs."

His gaze moved to Shannon. With her, he felt all of the things he felt with Autumn and so much more—attraction, passion, a fierce need to protect her.

"It always protects, always trusts, always hopes, always perseveres."

His love for her had never faded away. If anything, the years apart had allowed his heart time to heal while that love stayed buried deep down inside, lying dormant as he became the man God wanted him to be.

Shannon looked over the top of her camera and locked eyes with him.

"Love never fails."

Now was the time for love to bloom again.

The newlyweds celebrated long into the evening at Frederik Meijer Gardens. They danced and kissed and mingled and ate cake. They made out on the dance floor. They even snuck away for an hour alone while people were dancing. "To change" was all Chase had said. They were so obvious and so adorably in love.

An hour before sunset—the golden hour as photographers often called it—the bridal party went for a walk with Shannon to take pictures by the waterfall and among the gardens and sculptures. They couldn't have asked for a more beautiful night for a wedding. A soft, warm breeze caressed them, while deep shades of orange, red, and yellow painted the sky.

As they returned to the building after their photo session, Micah held back to walk with Shannon behind the group.

"How much longer will you be shooting?"

She tucked a stray hair behind her ear and tightened the elastic around her ponytail. "I normally stop after the bouquet toss, but it's Keely. I want to get as much of this for her as I can. She needs these pictures to remember every happy moment, especially after the day she's had."

The hair she had tucked fell again, fluttering softly in the wind. She was so pretty like that—so natural—and his mind flashed back to their kiss.

"Do I have something on my face?" she asked.

"Huh?"

"You're staring." She wiped at her cheek then her mouth as if to clear away some unknown crumb.

"I could stare at you all day." He wasn't going to hold back anymore. No matter how she reacted.

Her gaze shifted to the Children's Garden as they passed by.

When they reached the building, he held the door for her.

"Thanks." She gave him a little smile and began to veer toward the banquet room.

Micah slipped his hand around hers and tugged her in the opposite direction.

"I should get back to the reception," she told him.

"Have you been in here yet?" He tilted his head toward the tropical conservatory as he walked backwards, tugging on her hand.

She shook her head. "Not this time, but I've been here before, Micah."

"Just for a minute," he begged, giving her his best pouty expression.

She rolled her eyes. "A minute."

He didn't let go of her hand and led her through the sliding doors into the steamy room filled with lush tropical plants, colorful birds, streams, and waterfalls. They walked along the path that wrapped around the room, taking in the sights and smells of the flowers.

"I was here last year for the butterflies," she told him. "Every spring, the whole place is filled with them. It's beautiful."

He came to a stop in the middle of a small bridge. *"You're beautiful."*

Her eyes met his, her lips parted, and he couldn't help himself. He slid his arms around her waist and pulled her as close as he could with her equipment on her hip and lowered his lips to press against the softness of her cheek. "I can't stop thinking about that kiss this morning," he whispered.

A sigh escaped her lips as her eyelids slid closed.

His lips touched her forehead, her other cheek, the tip of her nose. She opened her eyes and tilted her chin up, poised and ready.

He leaned in slowly, his nose brushing against hers, only a breath away.

"Hey, you two," one of the groomsmen called from the doorway. "Sorry to interrupt, but they need you, Shannon. Keely's about to toss the bouquet."

Shannon's breath stuttered as she wriggled from Micah's hold. "Oh my gosh. Why do I keep letting this happen?" She bolted for the door.

He followed her along the path toward the exit. "Shannon."

She kept moving. "I have to do my job."

"I know, but we need to talk."

She glanced back over her shoulder at him, but didn't stop.

"Shannon, wait!"

"What is wrong with me?" The automatic doors slid open, and she walked through. "You have a girlfriend."

"No, I don't!"

Her feet came to a halt, and she looked over at him as he caught up. "What do you mean?"

"I tried to tell you this morning—"

"We need you, Shannon!" Becca was heading toward them then, clearly frantic.

"I'm coming." She started walking again in the direction of the reception hall. "Did you and Autumn break up?"

Micah fell into step beside her and shook his head. "I will explain. I promise. Please come find me before you leave, okay?"

She was unable to respond as Becca whisked her away to take pictures of the bouquet toss. Micah didn't pay much attention to that tradition playing out, only to Shannon photographing it all. He watched her work and prayed for his chance to tell her everything.

Micah sat on a bench outside the main entrance, staring up at the night sky. The stars were difficult to see with the glow from the city lights, but the brightest constellations showed through. He heard the sliding doors open behind him and felt Shannon's presence before she sat down next to him.

"Hey." She sounded weary.

He smiled over at her.

"Where's Autumn?" she asked.

"She left hours ago. Not much of a late night party kind of girl."

"Same. If it wasn't for weddings, I would never leave the house after ten o'clock."

"Sounds pretty good to me." He imagined late nights staying home with Shannon in his arms, snuggling on the couch, watching movies, tucking their kids in bed, making out and more until dawn. He shook away those thoughts before he got himself into trouble.

"So, what did you want to tell me?" Her eyes sparkled from the street lights.

"I thought you should know that Autumn and I ... our relationship isn't what you think."

Her eyebrows wrinkled and squeezed together in confusion. "What do you mean?"

"We're not dating in the traditional sense of the word."

Her face screwed up. "What does that even mean? You're either dating or you're not."

"We're not."

She looked more confused than when he first began. "I don't understand."

"It has to do with Jacquie. I know it seems she's still pretty crazy over our breakup, but she was even worse in the beginning. Autumn was there for it all. She and I have been friends since freshman year of college, and she saw how hard it was on me."

"And your friendship became more?"

He could tell she was trying to wrap her mind around what he was saying. "Autumn suggested we tell Jacquie she and I were dating to try to get her to finally realize it was over. But we've only ever been friends from the start."

"How long have you been"—she made air quotes—"dating?"

"About six months."

Her mouth dropped open a little. "So, she put her whole dating life on hold just for you? Are you sure she doesn't have feelings for you?"

"It's not like that. Never has been."

"Whose idea was it?"

"Hers." He realized now how it might appear to her. "Okay, I know what you're thinking, but her mother and grandmother are constantly hounding her about finding a guy to marry. This helped get them off her back for a while. It was a win-win for both of us."

Shannon didn't seem convinced. "I'm sorry, but have you seen you? No girl would devote so much time to a guy she saw no future with. No matter how good a friend you say she is. There's no way she did this without hoping your feelings for her might change."

Micah thought about that for a minute. Could it be true? Could Autumn feel more for him than she had said? She'd never hinted at that, but he suddenly felt unsure. Women were a mystery sometimes. Could he have misread her?

"And what about you? Do you have feelings for her?"

"Only friendship."

Shannon sighed. "Why couldn't you just let me go on believing you two were in a real relationship? What difference does it make now?"

He shifted to face her more. "I didn't want you to feel guilty about our kiss at the church … or the almost kiss tonight, because I wasn't cheating on Autumn with you."

She chewed on her bottom lip. "It was just a kiss, Micah. It doesn't have to mean anything. We got caught up in the moment."

"It meant everything to me."

Her shoulders sank. "This is too hard. If we start talking about this right now, it's only going to make things harder."

He took her hand, and her eyes met his. They were filled with a sadness that made his heart ache. "Don't you think we've both grown up and changed enough that we could make it work this time?"

"Micah." Her eyes dropped to their hands, and she tried to pull hers away, but he kept a firm grip.

"Please, just let me say this. If you don't want to talk about it and you want to leave when I'm finished, then that's fine. But let me get this out."

Her eyes lifted to his then dropped as she nodded.

"I miss you. I've missed you for a decade. All this time, I wondered what you'd think of the life I've made for myself in Virginia. I wondered what it would be like if you had come with me when I asked. What kind of life we'd have right now. And I know maybe it's foolish of me to hold onto hope after all this time, because you ended it. You walked away from me. And I still don't know why, but I don't care anymore. I'm so sorry for whatever I did back then that caused you to break up with me. I was young and stupid, and if I could go back and have a do-over, I'd take it back—whatever it was—because I want you, Shannon. I'll never stop hoping and praying for another chance with you."

"Micah."

"I know you still feel something for me. Please don't try to deny it."

She stared at the ground in front of them until he took her face in his hands and tilted it up, forcing her eyes to meet his.

"I love you, Shannon McGregor. I always have, and I always will.

And I want you back. I want the life we talked about. You by my side. The house full of kids. All of it."

Tears were streaming down her cheeks then, and he kissed them away.

"Don't cry, love."

She removed his hands and turned away from him. Her shoulders shook as she sobbed.

"Shannon, what is it?" He took hold of her shoulders and tried to turn her to him, but she wiggled out of his grasp.

"It can't happen," she whimpered.

"Why not?" His throat tightened with tears of his own.

"I can't give you what you want." She started to stand, but he gently took hold of her arm.

"Please talk to me."

She sat back down and faced him.

"I don't know what you think you can't give me. All I want is *you*," he repeated.

"You want the dream, Micah." She brushed her tears aside and looked him in the eye. "But I can't give you that, because I can't have kids."

Chapter 20

Those four words were not what he had expected to come out of Shannon's mouth. "You can't have kids?"

She brushed away more tears.

"How do you know?"

"I have PCOS. It's Polycystic Ovary Syndrome."

"What does that mean?" he asked.

"I get cysts on my ovaries sometimes. I used to have a lot of problems with my periods, where I either wouldn't get them for months or they would last for a really long time with a lot of pain and excessive bleeding." She made a face. "Sorry if that's an overshare."

"No, I want to know everything."

"Long story short, my hormone and insulin levels are messed up. That's why you saw all the greens in my fridge. People with PCOS can gain a lot of excess weight. Eating healthy helps prevent my body from doing that and from turning diabetic."

"So this means no kids?"

"My body doesn't release eggs like it's supposed to. My doctor said I am very unlikely to conceive the old-fashioned way." She lowered her head, almost looking ashamed.

"But you could?"

"The diet is supposed to help women who are trying to conceive have a more healthy ... environment. But if the eggs aren't there, well ... no baby. Plus, I'm on the pill to regulate the periods, so yeah, I can't really get pregnant if I'm on the pill."

It was all starting to make sense now. "Wouldn't you just stop taking the pill if you wanted to get pregnant?"

"The pills have helped so far. I was pretty miserable before, Micah. It sometimes went on for weeks, and I got really weak at times. I'm afraid of going through that again."

He remembered how she used to get bad cramps and stay home from school for days. But she had always downplayed it. He never knew it had been this bad for her.

"What are the scars on your stomach?"

"I had a large cyst and had laparoscopic surgery to remove it."

He took in a deep breath and let it out, suddenly scared at the thought of something being wrong with her. "This isn't life threatening, right?"

"It can be. I'm at a higher risk for diabetes and some kinds of cancer."

His heart skipped a beat. "But you're okay?"

"I'm okay."

The pieces suddenly fell into place.

"How long have you known?"

It seemed like an eternity passed while Micah waited for her to answer, and he realized he already knew the answer, even before she spoke the words.

"How long, Shannon?"

"I was diagnosed in August of 2001," she whispered.

His head dropped back, and he looked up at the night sky, biting the inside of his cheek to stop himself from crying. This was what he had wanted to know all of these years. This was it. The reason she had broken up with him. He wasn't sure what to say or do. His instinct was to take her in his arms and kiss her and tell her it would all be okay. But another part of him wanted to lash out. She had made this choice alone, without giving him all of the facts. Would it have changed things? There was no way to know how he would've reacted back then, but now ...

The anger won out over the urge to comfort. "How could you not tell me? How could you keep something that important from me?"

"You don't know how hard this was," she mumbled.

"No, I don't, because you didn't care enough to let me share the burden with you. You decided. On your own. That's not love."

"Of course it is."

He gritted his teeth as he stood and paced back and forth.

"I loved you enough to let you go." Her cheeks were soaked with tears. "You had a better chance of having your dreams come true without me."

"You don't know that. Did you not hear a word I said to you? You were always with me. All these years. I could've been here for you. We would've gotten through this."

"I come from a big family, Micah. A gigantic family tree with tons of branches on both of my parents' sides. And it kills me to know my branch of the tree stops with me. I'm like a dead stub sticking off a larger branch, an ugly eyesore, while all the other branches grow and flourish around mine."

"Shannon." He sat down beside her again.

"And you ... are you willing to let your family tree stop with you? It's only you, Micah. It's just you and your aunt, and you wanted this big family with lots of kids for us to raise and love and ..." She broke down then.

The instinct to hold her kicked in, and he did just that.

She cried into his chest, gripping the jacket of his tuxedo. "I can't give you the family you want," she whimpered.

His heart ached. He did want a family. A huge one. He wanted kids, and he wanted them with her. A part of him and a part of her. So many times he had pictured beautiful raven-haired daughters with brown eyes like their mother's and cute little towheaded boys like him running around causing all sorts of trouble.

"I wanted that with you. So much. I wanted a son to carry on my name, but—"

"But I'm broken. I'll never be able to give you that, Micah. I can't be what you need." She pulled away and scrambled to her feet. "I can't do this anymore. It hurts"—her words were interrupted by a sob— "too much." And she took off across the parking lot.

"Shannon!" He wanted to race after her and tell her it didn't matter, but he couldn't bring himself to stand. A jumble of confused thoughts whirled around in his mind. As much as he loved Shannon, the idea of never creating a child together was painful. It had been one of their biggest dreams, more important than career or any other detail they had dreamed up for their life. He wanted to tell her that they didn't need kids. The love he had for her was so strong, but would it be enough? Would it get them through the times when the desire for children was overwhelming? And what if they decided to try? He knew if he asked, she would do it for him. But would that cause her physical pain? He couldn't bear that. And what of the disappointment they would face with each negative test result?

This was by far the most difficult thing he had ever faced. And she'd been dealing with this—holding onto this secret—for years. He hated that he'd hurt her tonight, that he'd forced her to talk when she'd wanted to leave well enough alone.

So he let her go, he let her walk away, to cry and think and grieve. Because that's exactly what he needed to do.

Chapter 21

What Shannon needed more than anything after the emotionally draining week she'd had was to be home. She couldn't wait to embrace her mother and hide there in her arms for a while. No matter what was happening in her life, a hug from Mama always made it better.

When she arrived at her parents', she had to park Duncan's car on the street because there were several extra cars in the driveway. Shannon looked at herself in the rearview mirror and sighed. Makeup could not hide the puffiness around her eyes from crying herself to sleep.

The truth was out. Finally. And it felt like a burden had lifted, it really did. But it still hurt, seeing the look on his face, knowing she couldn't give him what he wanted, what he needed in this life. He loved her still, she knew he did. But it wasn't enough. She had known it then, and his reaction had only confirmed that letting him go had been the right thing. She had to accept that and trust in God's plan for her life from now on.

A car pulled up right behind hers. Shannon had been so focused on the wedding drama and Micah that she nearly forgot she'd invited Jamie over for Sunday dinner.

Jamie practically bounced out of her car, dressed in a cute little off-the-shoulder dress in a burgundy floral that blended well with the streaks in her hair and showed off half of the tattoo of a vintage 1950s Canon camera on the back of her right shoulder.

Shannon whistled. "You look nice."

Jamie's deep wine-colored lipstick accentuated the fullness of her lips, and her eyes popped with the mascara and smoky eyeshadow she wore. "I like to look my best."

"For my brother," Shannon teased.

"I mean ..." Jamie fluffed her hair a little. "Bonus if he thinks I look good."

Shannon couldn't help but smile. Those two were so obvious sometimes. She wondered if either of them would ever get serious about settling down and realize how right they could be together. She would be thrilled to have Jamie as her sister. But she didn't want to get ahead of herself. It had been awkward being subjected to Keely's matchmaking, and she would never try to play Cupid and push Duncan and Jamie together. If it happened, it would have to happen naturally. Still, she held onto hope that her brother and her best friend could find happiness someday. Even better if they found it with each other.

Jamie walked over and hugged her. "Looks like you had a very long day yesterday."

Shannon scrunched up her nose. "That obvious, huh? How awful do I look?"

"Not awful. Never that. Just tired."

"I'll fill you in on everything later." She walked to the back of her car and popped the trunk. "Oh, and guess what Micah found."

Jamie shrieked. "Our stuff!" She grabbed her cameras and bag from the trunk and moved it to her own vehicle. "I knew Micah was good for something."

Shannon forced a laugh. She shouldn't have mentioned his name. It hurt more than she expected.

The girls walked into the house and were hit with the aroma of Mama's homemade spaghetti sauce simmering in the kitchen.

"We're here!" Shannon announced.

Jamie inhaled deeply, her eyes slipping shut. "*Mmmm*, smells delicious."

"Cuore mio!" Mama came from the kitchen at the sound of her daughter's voice and pulled her into a warm embrace.

"Mama." She fought back tears and clung to her for dear life.

"Is everything okay?" Mama squeezed her tighter, holding on, letting her daughter be the one to pull away first.

"I just needed this." She kissed her mother on the cheek.

"Who's we?" Duncan stepped out of the kitchen behind Mama and spotted Jamie. Something about the way he looked at her seemed uncomfortable—almost awkward—which was the complete opposite of the way he normally looked at her. "I didn't know you were coming."

"Hello." A tall, slender brunette came up behind Duncan and slid her arms around his waist, her hands covered in oven mitts.

His arms came to rest on hers.

Shannon left her mother's embrace and turned in time to see Jamie's expression change from sweet and happy to complete shock.

"Shannon, Jamie ..." His voice stuck a bit on Jamie's name. "This is Dréa."

Dréa was gorgeous, and with her long, dark hair and deep, brown eyes, she already looked like a part of their family. Again, Shannon glanced at Jamie, who looked as if someone had slapped her across the face, and Duncan might as well have.

"Hi, I'm Duncan's sister, Shannon." She held her hand up in a little wave. "And this is my friend, Jamie."

"The photographers, right?" Dréa asked.

"Right."

"It's nice to meet you both." Her voice was smooth like silk. "Duncan's told me so much about you."

"Dréa," Nana called from the kitchen. "Can you come help me?"

"Coming, Nana," she replied and headed to the kitchen with Mama on her heels.

"Nana?" Jamie blurted.

Duncan's eyes flitted from Jamie's to Shannon's and back and forth again. "I told you I brought a surprise."

"That's not the surprise I thought you were talking about. I thought you brought me a sweatshirt or a coffee mug or something."

Duncan looked at Jamie then. "I'm sorry, Jame. I didn't know you were coming. I just ..."

Shannon had never seen her friend cry before, but Jamie looked darn close to bursting into tears at any moment.

Duncan awkwardly turned and walked back into the kitchen.

Jamie let out a breath she had obviously been holding. "I think I lost my appetite."

"Come on, don't let that bother you. It probably won't last."

Jamie raised an eyebrow at her. "How often has Duncan brought a girl home?"

She had a point. The answer was never. He'd dated casually for the most part, but hadn't once brought someone to the house.

"Come on, girls," Mama called. "Time to eat."

When they walked into the dining room, it was empty.

"We're eating outside today."

Shannon could see through the dining room window that there were tables set up to make one long table in the backyard and several family members were out there. "Did I miss something? Is this a family reunion?"

Mama laughed. "We're welcoming Duncan home."

"He hasn't been gone for *that* long."

When her mother left the room, Jamie touched Shannon's arm. "Maybe I shouldn't be here. It's like a family thing."

"Stop it. You're family to me."

Jamie barely managed a smile and hesitantly followed her into the backyard.

Shannon was pleased to see her Uncle Gene and Aunt Joanna, as well as their son, Maxwell, in attendance. Though they lived within an hour of each other, they only saw each other a few times a year.

"Hey, Max," Shannon greeted him.

His expression brightened, and he strode across the yard to hug her. "Hey, cuz, how are you?"

"Doin' okay. You?"

He shrugged. "Eh." His deep green eyes fell on Jamie. "Who's your friend?"

"This is Jamie." She looked at her friend, whose eyes were fixed on Duncan and Dréa standing across the yard, lip-locked. "Jamie, this is my cousin, Max."

Jamie startled and shifted her attention to the man in front of them. "Nice to meet you." She shook his outstretched hand.

Shannon could tell she was preoccupied, so she guided her to a seat at the table next to Nana. Max sat down on her other side.

Nana smiled up at Shannon. "Micah's not with you today?"

"Not today, Nana." She leaned down and kissed her grandmother on the cheek.

Seated on the other side of Nana was her sister, Pauline, who winked when Shannon sat down across from them.

Shannon noticed the large bowl of spaghetti in the center of the table and wished she could heap a pile onto her plate. She reached into the bowl and snuck a single noodle, slurping it slowly into her mouth. Mama was suddenly behind her with a plate of grilled chicken and steamed vegetables. Shannon looked up at her mother, who gave her a knowing smile and set the plate before her.

Papa took the head of the table with Mama to his right. Dréa took the seat Sophia normally would've sat in next to Mama with Duncan seated beside her. Leo and Paolo, cousins on Mama's side of the family, sat down across from Duncan, and Paolo stretched his long body diagonally across the table to high-five Shannon. Out of the many cousins they had, these two had always been frequent fixtures around their house.

The meal was delicious and the small talk plentiful, but for their usual Sunday dinner, it was quieter than normal. Maybe because there was an outsider at their table. Maybe it was the tension between Duncan and Jamie. Whatever the reason, it seemed a little off.

When the last noodle was slurped and the last wine sipped, Duncan stood slowly, glancing around the table with uncertainty. Shannon noticed the way his eyes skipped past Jamie.

"Uh, I have something ..."

Shannon had never seen her brother so nervous before.

"I have an announcement to make."

Shannon's stomach dropped, thinking about her best friend's feelings, hoping this announcement was about his job or anything other than what she feared it was.

"Dréa and I are engaged."

Dréa beamed and held her hand up to reveal a giant round diamond engagement ring.

Mama and Nana covered their mouths with their hands.

"Oh, my dear," Nana said, "you're good at keeping secrets. Just like your Nana."

His smile appeared forced and insincere, and he still avoided making eye contact with Jamie.

"It was hard not wearing the ring the whole time I've been here," Dréa told them.

The elder women of the family stood and walked around the table to hug on Duncan and Dréa.

Shannon glanced over at Jamie as a tear slid down her cheek.

"I'm gonna go," Jamie whispered across the table, and she stood and bolted from the yard before Shannon could stop her.

Shannon's eyes met Duncan's, and she gave him a look of disapproval as she, too, left the table.

Duncan followed her into the house. "Shan."

She looked back at him.

"Can you please tell her I'm sorry she found out like this."

"What is the deal with you two?"

He seemed extremely unnerved. "Nothing."

"Then why does it matter if she found out at all?"

"I don't know. I just … I know I've hurt her, and that kills me."

There was laughter and chatter coming from the yard, and Shannon looked from her brother to the door and back. "Who is this girl you're marrying? You just met her."

"I know … but sometimes you just know."

"And with her, you know?"

He nodded.

Shannon's eyebrow lifted. "Then why are you so worried about Jamie?"

"Just please make sure she's okay." He gave her a pointed look and motioned toward the front door. "Please."

Shannon rolled her eyes and walked outside in time to see Jamie's car pull into the street and drive away.

It took several knocks before Jamie's apartment door opened to reveal her puffy red eyes and tear-stained cheeks. She couldn't remember ever seeing Jamie cry. And it broke her heart that her usually confident friend had been brought to tears by her brother.

"Oh, Jamie." She hugged her friend tightly and let her cry. And this was a serious cry—the kind from the depths of the soul—where every tear bottled up is finally set free.

"You didn't have to come here, Shannon," she murmured. "You should be celebrating your brother's engagement." She could barely get those last two words out before more tears slid down her cheeks.

"He's an idiot," Shannon declared. "A total idiot."

"We already knew that much." A glimmer of Jamie's usual spunky personality showed through, which gave Shannon some comfort.

Jamie walked to the couch and climbed under a blanket.

Shannon followed, passing a large trash bag propped up against the coffee table and piles of tissues everywhere. It was clear by the wet, splotchy fabric that Jamie had been crying into the pillow at the end of the couch. She sat down opposite Jamie, turning with legs crossed to face her. "Can you please explain something to me?"

"What?" Jamie sniffled.

"What is it between you and my brother?" she asked. "I mean, you two have always been flirty, but lately, it seemed like there was more happening with you two. Am I wrong?"

"You're not wrong." Jamie swallowed hard and stared down at her hands. "Something happened. Before he left for Denver."

"What happened?"

It took Jamie a full minute before she spoke again, and even then, she wouldn't look Shannon in the eye. "We slept together."

Shannon's mouth fell open. "Excuse me? You slept together? As in ... you had sex with my brother?"

Jamie nodded, looking ashamed.

Her brother hadn't saved himself for marriage, this she knew, but years ago when he had given his life over to Jesus, he had told her he wanted to change and wait for the right girl, that he was planning to abstain until he found the woman he would marry. So to hear he had gone there with her best friend was more than a little shocking.

"Remember that night we were hanging out here, watching movies?"

Shannon nodded.

"You left early, but he stayed. We were flirting, as usual, and I dared him to kiss me. I never thought he'd actually do it. But once we started, we couldn't stop. We didn't want to stop." Tears sprung to her eyes again. "It was the best night of my life."

Jamie's sad little whimper broke Shannon's heart.

"I really thought this was it, that we were finally gonna make a go of it after all our flirting, but then he left for Denver."

"And what happened?"

"He didn't call me. I thought he would. He said he would. He left before I even woke up, and the first time I saw him since was two days ago when he dropped you off at the church."

"I can't believe him!" Shannon was appalled that Duncan would do that. It infuriated her that he could be the kind of guy to hook up with a girl and then blow her off. "I'm so angry right now. I want to give him a piece of my mind and let his new fiancée know exactly what kind of guy he is."

"You don't mean that. He's your brother, and you love him. Even if he did something like this."

She didn't know what to do, but she knew Jamie was right. She loved her brother, despite his flaws and mistakes—and this was a big one.

"It's not like I haven't had guys use me before." She lowered her head, and tears fell from her eyes and plopped onto her lap. "I just never thought Duncan would be one of them."

Shannon laid her hand on Jamie's.

"And I would normally be able to shake it off and move on if it wasn't for ..." Her shoulders began to shake again, and she buried her face in the pillow.

Shannon scooted closer and rubbed her back.

Jamie rotated her head and rested it on the pillow, looking up at Shannon. "I'm pregnant."

"You're pregnant?" Shannon swallowed hard.

A slow, sad nod was Jamie's answer.

The ache of sympathy in Shannon's heart spread through her and blended with a sudden flare of jealousy. Was this some kind of cruel joke? She might never have a child of her own and her friend had gotten pregnant without even trying.

"I thought I was late from the stress of wedding season or something, but then I remembered throwing up after the rehearsal dinner, so I took a test last night."

"And it was positive?"

"Yeah, I kind of freaked out and smashed some things." She pointed to the trash bag. "And then I thought, it's Duncan. We could do this. We could raise a baby together. So, I planned to tell him after lunch today." Her face screwed up as the emotions hit her again. "I don't know what to do now," she whimpered. "I don't know if I should keep it."

A strong instinct to protect the baby took over. "It's not the baby's fault you and Duncan got carried away. That's my brother's baby, Jamie. Please, don't do anything without telling him."

"But he's getting married now. If I tell him, I'll mess up his whole life, and he'll resent me for it. And even if he were to leave her for me, it would be because of the baby, and I don't want him that way. I want him because he wants to be with me, and he obviously didn't or he would've called after that night."

"You'll never know unless you talk to him."

"It would be easier for everyone if I made it go away."

Shannon couldn't breathe. The thought of Jamie getting rid of the baby filled her with a sense of panic. "Of course, it would be easier on Duncan if you terminated the pregnancy and never told him. But what about you? Could you go back to your life and pretend it never happened?"

"I don't know. This isn't how I thought things would go down with me and Duncan. And honestly, if he and I were a couple, I'd want this baby. But I don't want to be a single mom. I know that."

Shannon could no longer hold back tears.

Jamie sat up then. "Are you mad at me?"

Shannon wiped at her wet cheeks. "In our family, we believe every life counts, that God has a purpose for each person, including the babies not yet born, no matter how they came to be conceived. This baby is innocent, and it's our blood. A part of our family."

A hint of a smile touched Jamie's lips. "You have no idea how long I've wanted to be part of your family."

"You *have* to tell him, Jame. You don't know what might happen when you do. Because no matter who this girl is he brought home, he cares about you. I know it. You should've seen his face when you left. He was so worried about you. He made me promise to check on you and make sure you were okay."

"Really?"

"Really."

Jamie shook her head. "No, I can't hold onto false hope. How would I do this on my own? I don't have any family here. I can't afford a nanny or day care. Not to mention the cost of actually having the baby. Doctor appointments. Food. Diapers."

Shannon could sense that Jamie was working herself into a frenzy. "Our family would help. You know we would."

"I don't know what to do." Jamie covered her face and cried some more.

"I'm here for you," Shannon assured her. "You're my best friend, and I want you to be happy." She squeezed her eyes, fighting back tears of her own. "But Duncan is my brother, and if you don't tell him, I can't promise that I won't."

Jamie's eyes grew as big as saucers. "What? Shannon, come on."

"He has the right to know."

Jamie scrambled up from the couch and stared at her. "Please don't do that. Not yet anyway."

"Are you going to tell him?"

"Yes."

"Before or after?" Shannon couldn't hide the edge of anger in her voice. And when Jamie didn't reply right away, Shannon didn't hold back. "You're going to do it, aren't you?"

"I don't think I have any other choice."

"You do have choices. Don't do anything rash."

"I can do whatever I want. It's my body."

"That's true. And I can sit here and tell you what I hope you'll do and the way I hope things will turn out, but there are no guarantees. I don't know how Duncan will react when he finds out ... and he will find out. Whether it's from you or me."

Jamie made a face.

"If you end this pregnancy and he finds out after the fact, he might never forgive you."

Jamie stared at the floor.

"But here's another option for you to consider." Shannon breathed in and out deeply. "Adoption."

"I don't know."

"I want to adopt the baby," she blurted.

Jamie's eyes widened again. "Wait, what?"

"The reason I broke up with Micah all those years ago was because I found out I can't have kids. He wanted a big family. It was a dream of ours. So I let him go so he could have that with someone else."

"Oh, Shannon."

"It breaks my heart that you're going through this right now, Jamie." The tears filled her eyes again. "I'm so sorry my brother was so careless with you and your feelings. But if you don't want it, and if he doesn't want it, I will be this baby's mom. I want children. I always have. And if I can raise a baby that's biologically part of our family, I would be so honored to do that. You can be part of its life and so can Duncan." Shannon didn't know where any of that had come from. She'd thought about adoption over the years, but could she really raise her brother's baby as her own? She was certain if Duncan knew, he would move heaven and earth for this child. There was no way he wouldn't want to know about and raise this baby. So, while there was a part of her that was serious and would take responsibility for the baby if nobody else would, she really wanted Jamie to consider all her options before she did something she couldn't take back.

"I don't know what to say."

"Please, think about it, okay?"

"I will."

"And please talk to Duncan."

Jamie simply nodded in reply.

Shannon didn't know if she'd gotten through to her at all. She hoped she had, and as she left the apartment and drove back toward her parents' house, she prayed.

"God, please hear me. I know I haven't really talked to you for a long time, and I'm so sorry for that. I pray you'll forgive me and hear me now, because I need you. Jamie and Duncan need you. Their baby needs you." A sob hit her as she became suddenly overwhelmed by their situation and by her own pain. "If you want me to raise that baby, I will. Even if I'm meant to do it alone. Is that why all of this is happening? Is their baby meant to fill the hole in my heart from the babies I'll never have? Because I believe what Maggie said yesterday. I believe you have a plan for us and you've got the big picture view we just don't have. I believe you're working all things together for our good. Please show me your will for me. For all of us." Tears flowed down her cheeks. "And please ... please let Jamie keep the baby."

Chapter 22

Shannon thinks you have feelings for me." Micah hated bringing it up as he drove Autumn to the airport to catch her flight home. Autumn snorted.

"She doesn't think a girl would sacrifice her dating life to help out a guy without hoping it will turn into more." Micah glanced over at her to gauge her reaction.

Her eyes widened, and it appeared as if she might burst out laughing any minute. "Oh, seriously? She's been reading too many romance novels."

"She's not much of a reader. Movies are her thing."

"Well, too many romantic comedies then. Either way, she couldn't be more wrong."

"Gee, thanks."

"Don't get me wrong. You're an attractive guy, Micah. But I've always seen you as more of a brother, and that hasn't changed since we started all this."

"Are you sure?"

"You know I am." Autumn was the most honest person he knew. She never lied, and he knew she wasn't starting now.

He'd already known the truth before he had broached the subject, but he wanted to be completely certain. The last thing he ever wanted to do was lead her on or hurt her, because when their fake relationship ended, he wanted their friendship to remain intact.

"Are you ready to end this passionate affair of ours?" she teased.

He shook his head. "No."

"No?"

"Jacquie's still ... well, still being Jacquie."

"What about Shannon?"

"I told you, she doesn't want me."

Autumn gave him a disapproving look. "She didn't say that, now did she?"

"Not those exact words."

"Her sacrifice is admirable, really. She wants you to be able to have the family you always wanted. She wants you to be happy, and she's willing to walk away to give you the freedom to have that with someone else."

"But I only ever wanted to have a family with *her*."

"Then tell her that. There are lots of kids out there that need good homes. Adopt some babies. Have a family that way."

It sounded so simple when Autumn said it. But would Shannon want that? Would she be open to adopting? They'd only ever talked about biological children. She'd talked about what it would feel like to carry a baby. Would raising a child she hadn't carried be too difficult for her? There were so many things he still wanted to say to her, conversations like this they needed to have.

"You don't have to park," Autumn said as he switched lanes toward the short-term parking lot.

"Huh?"

She pointed toward the other lane. "Just drop me off at the terminal."

"What kind of boyfriend would I be if I let you carry your own bags in?"

"The fake kind." She winked at him.

He laughed.

"Go talk to her." She laid her hand on his arm. "Before your flight tonight. You know you want to."

She knows me so well.

Chapter 23

When Shannon returned to her parents', she found the family still gathered in the backyard, talking and laughing, enjoying the fresh air and each other's company. Dréa seemed like one of the family already, chatting with Nana and Great Aunt Pauline like they'd known each other forever.

Shannon wandered over to stand behind her dad, who smiled up at her when she laid her hands on his wide, solid shoulders.

"I'm an on-air radio personality," Dréa explained. "I'm on a morning show with another DJ on a Christian music channel."

"Like that Delilah?" Nana asked.

They all laughed.

"Not really," Dréa answered. "I don't have my own show or the kind of following she has. Maybe someday."

Dréa definitely had the voice for radio, and Shannon could see how her brother could fall in love with it and her so quickly. The whole family seemed enthralled with her too.

Shannon stared at Duncan until she finally made eye contact, tilting her head toward the house.

Duncan patted Dréa on the knee as he stood. She kept talking as he walked toward Shannon.

They went into the kitchen, and Duncan went straight for a tin of cookies and started munching on one of the chocolate chip variety.

"You slept with her?"

Shannon's question caught him by surprise and caused him to choke on a chunk of cookie. She patted his back with little vigor, knowing he wasn't actually choking.

"How could you do that and then get engaged to someone else in two months' time?"

He coughed once more before his head fell forward in shame. "She told you."

"Of course she told me. She's heartbroken, Duncan. How did you think she would feel?"

His eyes shot to the back door. "Keep your voice down."

"You didn't tell your fiancée?"

He made a face at her.

"How could you, Duncan? Really, shame on you. I never thought you'd be that guy—hooking up and sneaking out before the sun comes up." She wanted to scream at him, to tell him Jamie was pregnant, but she had to give Jamie a chance to give him that news.

"Is that what she said?" He shook his head adamantly. "I had to catch my plane."

"No, she didn't say you snuck out. I put the pieces together."

"That's not what happened at all. I stayed with her as long as I could. I didn't want to leave her."

"Why didn't you call her from Denver then? If you really care about her, why blow her off?"

His shoulders drooped. "Once I walked out of that apartment, I felt so guilty. I wasn't going to do that again until I got married, but I was always so attracted to her." He glanced toward the door again and kept his voice low. "She's such a cute, feisty little thing, and the second I kissed her, I knew I was lost. I was so strong for so long, but I lost the battle. And I was ashamed. I felt like I took advantage of her. She wasn't mine to have, but I had her anyway. And I didn't know how to tell her that without hurting her. What girl wants to hear afterwards that the guy feels anything but happy and content and ... and in love, and I couldn't tell her those things."

"And walking away without any explanation was the answer?"

He ran his hands over his face and pushed his hair back off his forehead. "I don't know."

"I've spent ten years second-guessing my decision to break up with Micah, wondering how different life would be now if I'd told him the truth from the start. Don't make the same mistake I made. Tell her the truth, Duncan. She deserves to hear it."

"I can't look into those big brown eyes of hers and tell her that. I can't be near her and not want her still."

"Duncan." For as close as she was to her brother, this was not what she'd expected him to say. "You can't marry Dréa if this is the way you feel." He was obviously struggling, and she was hopeful that Duncan might actually want to be with Jamie.

"We can't base a relationship on physical attraction. And that's what it would be. I like Jamie. I always have. But when it comes right down to it, we don't know that much about each other. It's always been a pretty surface relationship. We goof around and flirt. We don't have deep conversations. I don't know anything about her family. I don't know how she became a photographer. Heck, I don't even know her middle name, and I knew all those kinds of things about Dréa after the first date."

"So get to know her." Shannon knew what a wonderful person Jamie was, and she could see the possibility of something more serious between her and Duncan.

"My desire for her isn't a good enough foundation for a relationship. We may be sexually compatible—"

Shannon held up her hand. "Too much information."

"But we have nothing else in common," he continued. "We don't share the same beliefs. It would never work."

If only he knew the whole story. If only he knew Jamie might be connected to him and their family for the rest of their lives because he couldn't control his desire for her.

"It was a mistake." He said the words she hoped he wouldn't say, because she knew if Jamie had been there to hear him say it, she would've been even more devastated than she already was. And hearing that might be enough to push her toward getting rid of the baby.

"Please, go talk to her. She deserves that much."

Just as Duncan let out a groan, there was a knock on the door. He looked all too happy to escape the conversation with Shannon to answer it.

Shannon grabbed one of the cookies from the tin and stared at it. It'd been a while since she'd had a chocolate chip cookie. What did it matter now anyway? The cookie touched her lip as Micah stepped into the kitchen with a small bouquet of wildflowers in his hand.

"I hope these are still your favorite." Micah approached and handed over the bouquet.

Shannon dropped the cookie onto the counter and took the flowers. Her heart warmed at his thoughtfulness. And then she gave her brother a piercing stare she hoped spoke a thousand words.

Duncan replied with a weak grin and left them alone.

"I was hoping we could talk. I don't want to make this harder for you, but I think there's more to say." He nodded toward the back door. "If I'm interrupting ..."

She shook her head as she grabbed the cookie and took a gigantic bite. "Take me away from here."

The two of them walked to Micah's car, and she couldn't help but remember Wednesday morning when he came to pick her up on the side of the highway. It felt like so much had changed in the span of four days.

"Where to?" he asked.

"Let's go to Aunt Pauline's."

"Is everything okay?" he asked as he drove toward the lake house.

Shannon blew out an exasperated breath. "Not really."

"I thought I picked up on something between you and Duncan."

She shook her head. "You have no idea."

"Wanna talk about it?"

"Maybe later."

They rode in silence until they pulled into Aunt Pauline's driveway. Micah got out and headed for the front door, but Shannon motioned for him to follow her along the side of the house.

"She's not home. She's at our house, actually."

"Oh." He glanced around the yard. "Will she mind if we're here?"

"She's always saying 'my house is your house.'"

They walked across the lawn—the same lawn where they'd spent those Fourth of Julys during their relationship. When they reached the dock, Shannon kicked off her sandals. Micah did the same, and they sat and dropped their feet into the water.

Micah sat close enough that Shannon could feel the heat radiating from his arm, but not close enough that they were touching. She was grateful for that, because she wasn't sure she could handle him touching her right now. Everything still felt so raw and exposed, especially after the news from Jamie this morning. She was dying to tell Micah, to have someone to talk to about it. But she wasn't sure she should share Jamie's secret.

Micah suddenly let out a little chuckle.

She looked over at him. "What's funny?"

"I was just thinking about the last time we were here. How I threw you off this dock." He had thrown her over his shoulder and carried her across the yard to prove he would in fact throw her in the lake if she didn't stop picking on him for the way he placed the food on his plate—foods just were not meant to touch, in his opinion, even though Shannon's Great Aunt Betty had told him it all went the same place in the end.

The memory came rushing back, and she laughed. "I like to remember the part that came after you threw me in."

The corner of his mouth lifted. "Yeah, that was fun."

Making out in the lake while the fireworks lit the night sky above them. Yeah, that was a memory she liked to think would remain clear and strong in her mind.

His expression turned serious. "I'm leaving for Virginia tonight."

That wasn't what she thought he would lead with, but she knew it was coming. She knew he was going home soon. The wedding weekend was over, and it was time to return to his real life.

"With Autumn?"

"She had an earlier flight."

Shannon skimmed her foot across the surface of the water.

"You were wrong about her."

She looked over at him again.

"She doesn't have feelings for me. I asked her point blank, and I know her. She would never lie to me. I asked that of her from the start, and she knows how I feel about honesty in relationships."

Shannon winced.

"That wasn't a jab at you. I understand why you weren't honest with me, why you didn't tell me about your diagnosis back then. You were trying to give me the best life I could have, at least the life you thought you couldn't give me. But did you ever stop to think maybe it wasn't your decision to make?"

"Not at first," she replied sadly. "I thought it was the only way. That if I let you go, you could find happiness with someone else, someone who could give you the family you wanted."

He moved his arm and rested it on the dock behind her so it was against her back. A shiver moved over her body.

"I'm sorry you had to go through all that alone. If I had known, I would've been there for you every step of the way."

"Duncan brought me to the church the other day because I had an appointment with my doctor. Some abnormal cells came back in my regular exam. I was so scared, Micah."

He scooted closer, tucking her into his side. "What did the doctor say?"

"Everything's fine. She wanted to be safe rather than sorry." She glanced over at him then out at the lake. "The thing is, because I'm at a higher risk for certain cancers, I'm always worried this thing is going to kill me."

"You can't live your life in fear of something that probably won't happen."

She felt so safe and secure, tucked against him, sheltered from the world.

"I'm sorry I didn't tell you back then," she said quietly. "I was eighteen and overwhelmed with all the details about my diagnosis and what it meant for me. For us. So many couples break up over struggles with infertility, and I was scared that would happen to us. Not to mention the cost of fertility treatments if I couldn't get pregnant. And I was afraid of getting cancer. I thought I was making the right choice, saving you from having to deal with all of this."

He leaned over and kissed her temple. "You made the wrong choice, but I forgive you for it. And I want to make it all right again."

Her gaze settled on his brown eyes, a chunk of his blond hair hanging over one of them. She lifted her fingers and moved it out of the way before she could stop herself.

His hand slid up and circled her wrist, and she went still. "I thought a lot about things last night and all this morning, and I was wondering what you'd say if I asked you again to come to Virginia with me."

Did he just ask her that? He had to know what her answer would be. "Micah."

"It could be a new start."

"My answer would be the same. I'm sorry, Micah. My life is here. My business is here. And I can't leave Jamie right now."

His eyebrows narrowed. "Why not? She has her own business, and the studio building fell through, so you aren't locked into anything."

"Thanks for reminding me." She frowned.

"I didn't say it to hurt you. I'm just trying to understand what's keeping you here."

She wrestled with whether to tell him.

"Maybe you don't feel the same about me anymore, and if that's the case, I understand."

He looked so sad and vulnerable, like he had laid his heart out in front of her and she had smashed it to smithereens.

She leaned close until her lips were within a couple inches of his and looked him in the eye. "I feel the same." And then she closed the gap between them, pressing a soft kiss to the corner of his mouth.

His hands moved to either side of her face then, his lips gliding across hers, causing her heart to stutter in her chest. She tilted her head, opening her mouth to his, pouring everything she had into this kiss.

"Please," he whispered against her lips. "Please, come to Virginia."

"Jamie's pregnant," she breathed.

He angled away from her, looking shocked. "Oh."

"With my brother's baby."

His eyes widened as his mouth fell open. "Whoa! Drop a bombshell, why don't you."

"I know. And he came home from Denver with his new fiancée."

Micah looked flabbergasted. "What is happening right now? Is this for real?"

She nodded. "That's pretty much how I reacted too." She filled him in on all Jamie and Duncan had told her.

"Are you okay?" he asked her. "It couldn't be easy for you, hearing she's pregnant."

"I thought it had to be some kind of cruel joke. But it's not. And I'm so afraid she's going to get rid of it."

"Would she do that?" he asked.

Shannon shrugged. "She's really confused right now."

"Who could blame her?"

They got quiet, staring out at a boat passing by on the water.

Micah wound his fingers through hers and raised the back of her hand to his lips. "I'm not sure where things stand with us right now, and I don't want to leave for Virginia like this."

"It's okay, Micah. We're okay."

"I thought I'd come see you and talk to you and just know what to say if you turned Virginia down again, but I don't. I don't know what to say or do. I have a job I love, that I'm really good at. I go to a great church. I have my own home and friends who've become my extended family. But I don't want to leave you again."

"I get it. I'm glad you know everything now, but I'm not expecting anything from you. I didn't think you knowing would change anything. Don't feel bad about going home."

He kissed her temple and pulled her into a hug.

Shannon's throat tightened with impending tears. Deep in the recesses of her heart, she had clung to a hope that one day maybe if Micah knew the truth, he would tell her it didn't matter to him, that they could be happy without the house full of kids, that she was enough for him. She wanted to be all he needed to make him happy. But he didn't tell her that just now. He told her the opposite with the words left unspoken—that his family was in Virginia and it would never be her.

Chapter 24

The entire flight home, Micah hadn't been able to stop thinking about Shannon. His mind replayed the events of the week, every conversation, every moment he'd spent with her, and the truths he'd come to know. He loved his life in Virginia. He'd been happy there. At least he thought he had. But heading back there now without her felt wrong. His house would hold an emptiness it hadn't before, a gap only Shannon could fill.

He understood her reasons for saying no this time. He understood why she had ended things all those years ago. He also knew that Shannon still cared for him and that meant there might be hope of a life with her after all.

He should've told her that. He should've told her he didn't want a family with anyone but her. He should've asked what she thought about adoption. But once she'd said no to Virginia, he'd been confused. The whole situation was so confusing.

As he pulled up to his house, he wasn't happy to see Jacqueline sitting on the wicker chair on the front porch. He jumped out and marched right up to her, not bothering to grab his suitcase from the trunk.

She stood and held her hands up between them. "Before you say anything, please hear me out."

"Jacquie, you can't keep doing this."

"I came here to apologize."

His expression changed from annoyance to surprise.

"I'm not going to lie, Micah. I was disappointed that you didn't want to work things out."

159

"No, really?"

Her chin quivered a little. "You don't have to be so sarcastic all the time."

"Sorry, but you've made things more difficult than they needed to be. I heard you out the other night like you wanted. Why can't you just—"

"I'm letting you go, Micah." Jacqueline took a deep breath in and let it out.

His eyebrows raised.

"I never believed you and Autumn were in love, that you suddenly got together after being friends all those years." She shifted her weight from one foot to the other. "You told me so many times there was only friendship between you, that you weren't attracted to her in that way. It wasn't believable. I knew you were lying to me."

"I didn't know how else to get you to move on. You wouldn't take no for an answer."

"Because we were good together. Weren't we happy in the beginning?"

"Yeah, we had some happy times, but we just weren't right for each other. You weren't—"

"Shannon?" Jacquie spoke her name before he had a chance to. She nodded her head. "It was eye-opening seeing the two of you together, actually. The way you looked at her was different than any look you'd ever given me or Autumn. I could see how much you loved her without you saying a word."

"I've always loved her."

"That's why I came here today. So you and Autumn can stop your charade and you can be with Shannon."

Micah let out a little laugh. "If only it were that simple."

"Shouldn't it be?"

"There's a lot more to it. There are obstacles."

"*Pfft!* What obstacles can't be overcome when you love each other as much as the two of you?"

"Well, a big one is the fact that I live in Virginia and she lives in Michigan."

"Ask her to move here?"

"I tried that. She said no."

"Then move to Michigan. What else ya got?"

Micah laughed again. This didn't seem like the Jacqueline he'd come to know, the girl who'd practically stalked him for the past year. "Why are you being so great about this?"

"Because I know love when I see it. Everyone wants the kind of love you two have. And no matter what happened between us, I care about you and want you to be happy, Micah."

"Thank you, Jacquie. Truly." The urge to hug her overcame him, and he did just that.

She squeezed him tightly and wiped away tears when they parted.

"I'm sorry I hurt you," he told her.

"I know you are. And I'm sorry for how I've acted all these months." She gave him a little smile, then moved around him and down the porch steps to a car that had stopped in front of his house. She opened the door and looked back at him. "You should go get her, Micah."

And with that, she climbed in and the car disappeared down the street.

Micah sat down on the top step of his porch and shook his head. Part of him was unsure if that conversation had actually happened. But he couldn't stop thinking about what she'd said. There was no obstacle he wouldn't overcome for Shannon. He'd break down every wall in their way if he had to.

The first wall was location. That one was easy enough to remedy. He'd contact a realtor about selling his house. He'd go online and put some feelers out, see what kinds of computer engineering jobs were available in the Grand Rapids area. He loved his job at NASA, but he'd give it up in a minute to be with Shannon.

He thought about their other problem—her diagnosis. This one gave him pause. Not as easy to jump this gigantic hurdle, but there were options. He wished they could make a baby together. But if that couldn't happen, she would be enough for him. He smiled to himself as he came to that realization. Babies would be amazing, but Shannon would be his family, even without them.

But how could he make her believe he was okay with that?

His mind cycled through idea after idea until he pulled his phone from his pocket and dialed. "Chase, I need a favor."

Chapter 25

Sitting at her computer on Tuesday morning, an unfamiliar number came up on her phone. Most of the time this meant telemarketers, but this being both her personal and business number, she had to answer anyway.

"Shannon McGregor Photography."

"Hi there, Shannon, it's Vernon Howard."

This was unexpected.

"Hello, Vernon. What can I do for you today?" She wondered if he'd heard of another space for their business and if that might be the purpose of his call.

"Are you still interested in the studio space?" he asked.

She was confused. "I thought you sold it."

"The sale fell through."

A lump abruptly formed in her throat.

"I actually have another buyer interested, and they would like to make that studio space available to you."

Shannon gasped. "Are you serious?"

"As a heart attack," he said with a chuckle. "Can you meet me there in an hour?"

"Absolutely!"

"See you then."

She hung up and stared at the phone in disbelief. Did she just dream that? Was the studio a possibility for them after all? She couldn't help but smile, believing in her heart God had heard her on

Sunday. He was already working things out, already blessing her with things she hadn't even asked for.

Now, she could only hope her other prayer would be answered with the arrival of a little niece or nephew.

She dialed Jamie about the studio, but it went straight to voicemail. She left a quick message. Was Jamie hiding out because she didn't want to talk about the baby? For extra measure, she texted too.

When she got no reply, she decided to swing by the apartment and pick Jamie up on the way. It was nice to finally have her car back from the shop so she didn't have to rely on others to get her around.

At Jamie's apartment, she knocked several times without answer. Luckily, Jamie had given her an extra key in case of emergencies, so she let herself in.

"Jamie!" she called out.

Silence.

She glanced into Jamie's room, but it was empty, as was the bathroom.

Heading into the kitchen, she found a pen and notepad in one of the junk drawers and started to leave a note. If Jamie returned in the next hour, she could still meet her at the building. There was no way she would want to miss seeing this space—their space.

Just as she pressed pen to paper, she noticed an envelope on the end of the counter with her name written in thick, bold letters. She set the pen down and grabbed it. Inside was a torn off page from the same notepad she'd found in the drawer and a couple of camera memory cards—probably from Keely's shower and rehearsal.

I'm sorry I have to leave like this. I need time to decide.
Please don't tell Duncan.
- J

Shannon sank onto the nearest bar stool, and her heart squeezed so hard in her chest, she thought it might implode. Despite her prayers and everything she'd told Jamie, she had a strong feeling that when Jamie returned, she would no longer be pregnant. If only she could talk to her again, convince her. But once Jamie set her mind to something, she did it.

She yanked her phone out and started typing, barely able to see the screen through her tears.

"Please don't do anything you'll regret. Duncan has the right to know before you make any huge decisions. It's his baby too."

She paused typing and took a deep breath.

"And I was serious. If neither of you want it, I'll raise it as my own."

She didn't expect a reply, and she didn't get one.

Chapter 26

The studio space hadn't change since Simon moved out— modern, clean, stark white. But with a little paint and some renovations, they could warm it up and make it their own. Vernon held in his hand the paperwork for them to sign to seal the deal with the new owners. Oh, she wished Jamie was there for this moment.

"Is this amount correct?" Shannon asked. It was lower than the amount agreed upon with Vernon before, and it crossed her mind that, if Jamie didn't come back, she might still be able to afford it on her own.

Vernon shrugged his shoulders. "I'm just seeing to the details. You'll have to take it up with them."

Her eye caught on the name Pennington at the top of the agreement. *Pennington?* She crossed her arms over her chest. "Who exactly is buying this building from you?"

"I agreed to keep that confidential, but you'll meet them … very soon." Vernon chuckled.

"I think it needs a coat of paint. White walls feel so sterile," a familiar voice came from behind them.

Shannon spun around to find Micah standing in the middle of the space.

Her heart leapt. "What are you doing here?"

"I'm checking in on my investment," he replied as he glanced around the room.

"Did you get Chase to buy this building?" she asked, having recognized his friend's last name from the contract.

"We're partners," he said with a wink.

"Why? You both live and work in Virginia. Why would you buy a building in Michigan?"

He walked toward her and stopped a couple feet away, raising his arms out to the sides with palms up. "It's for you."

Shannon didn't know what to say.

"But it comes with a package deal. The building ... and me." He lowered his arms and took another step toward her. "I'm moving back."

She fought back tears at this news.

He tilted his head slightly to the right and his lips curved up. "Maybe we can't have everything we once dreamed of, but I wanted to give you this one. You needed a win."

It was no use. The tears were falling now.

Vernon left the space then, giving them some privacy.

"These are happy tears, right?" He took another step toward her.

She nodded and chewed on her bottom lip before launching herself at him, wrapping her arms around his waist, and burying her head in his chest. His lips pressed against the top of her head as his hands rubbed up and down over her back, and it was the most comforting thing she had felt in a long time.

"You have to know I would move mountains to make your dreams come true, right?" He spoke into her ear. "If I could somehow fix your body so we could have the children we always wanted, I would do it. I'd do anything for you."

She hugged him tighter, longing for more words, more of his thoughts.

"It's not easy, knowing we can never have a child of our own, because I want that more than I can put into words. But I can't go on with my life knowing that everything I believed all these years was wrong, that you didn't break up with me because you didn't love me, you did it because you loved me so much."

"I did," she mumbled as she lifted her head to look at him. "I do."

He rested his forehead against hers. "When I look at you, I see the beautiful, warm, funny, talented, passionate woman I fell in love with.

The woman I still love. You may not feel whole right now, but I want you to know that your diagnosis doesn't make you less of a woman in my eyes. It doesn't have to define our life. Maybe we'll never be able to make the big family we dreamed of. Maybe we'll find another way to have kids. But if not, you're enough for me." He lifted his head and gently took her face in his hands. "You're all I need, Shannon." He kissed the tip of her nose. "You'll be my family, and I'll be yours."

Tears slid down her cheeks and a smile lit up her face. "That's all I needed to hear."

Their lips met then, and if it hadn't been for Vernon outside wanting to lock up the building, they might have stayed there kissing all day, breathing life and hope into their relationship again, whispering renewed promises. Choosing love. Choosing each other.

Epilogue

December 2012

D o you like it?" Micah whispered in her ear. They looked out at the shining waters of Reeds Lake from the deck of a modest three bedroom home.

"You know I love the lake." She squeezed his arms tighter against her. "But lake houses aren't cheap. Can we really afford this?"

"*Mhmm.*" She felt him nod against her neck.

Shannon grew quiet as she stared out at the ripples the early winter wind was making across the surface.

Micah turned her to face him. "What is it?"

"Sometimes I can't believe this is happening. That after all our years apart, you weren't married to someone else. That you forgave me and took me back. I don't know what I did to deserve it."

He took her face in his hands. "How many times do I have to tell you, there's nobody else in this world for me but you."

She smiled up at him. "Same."

He took hold of her shoulders and rotated her to face the water again, his hands sliding around her, palms resting on her stomach. "How soon until you start showing?"

She shrugged and smoothed her shirt tightly across her belly. "I have a little bulge, don't you think?"

He laughed amusedly. "If you say so."

"I want to show so bad. I want everyone to know I've got our baby growing in here." She spun and threw her arms around him. Some days the happiness could not be contained. It bubbled up inside her until she was ready to burst or run through the neighborhood shouting with joy. She'd never been so happy. "This baby is a miracle."

"Our miracle."

"From God." They spoke in unison and started to laugh. It was what Nana had said every time she saw them after they made the announcement to the family.

Their little miracle from God.

Shannon didn't know if it was all her healthy eating over the years that had improved her chances of naturally conceiving. She was sure that had helped, but she and Micah knew the truth.

Shannon had become pregnant after only three months of trying—not years, as so many couples who struggled with infertility had to endure—and they truly believed God had made it happen for them. He had given them their dream of having a child together.

Maybe it would be their only child. Who knew how PCOS would affect her body going forward. But for now, she was going to take it easy and pray the pregnancy would be normal and end with a strong, healthy baby.

As they stood on the deck of what would soon be their home—another dream come true—she thought about the September night when they received the best news of their life.

"You're making me even more nervous than I already am," Shannon told Micah, who was pacing a hole in the carpet.

"How many minutes has it been?" He glanced at the clock in the kitchen once again.

"I set a timer. Come here and hold my hand."

He sat down beside her and took her hand in his just as the timer on Shannon's phone went off. They both jumped to standing and walked together to the bathroom, where the pregnancy test lay on the surface of the sink.

For the past few months, it had been a series of negative tests. Her periods had become irregular since she stopped taking birth control, making it easy to get their hopes up. But the one thing they decided before they were married was that she would stop taking the pill, and if she got pregnant the old-fashioned way, then great. And if not—if her cycle got too messed up again and caused her pain—then they weren't going to stress about it, and she would go back on them. They didn't want to go through the whole in vitro fertilization route, at least not at that early point in their marriage, so they left it up to nature and God.

"I can't look," Shannon said. "You look."

Micah picked up the test. "Okay, so two lines means pregnant and one means not pregnant, right?"

"Right," she gazed at him hopefully.

He pressed his lips together. "One line."

Her shoulders sank. "Okay." She nodded over and over as if to convince herself this was all right. "It's okay."

He touched her chin to get her to look at him. "I love you."

She grinned over at him. "I love you too."

He leaned in and kissed her on the tip of the nose. "Annnd ... a second line."

She jerked back and stared at him. "What?"

"Two lines." A huge smile spread across his face.

"Micah!" She smacked him on the arm and yanked the test from his hand. Sure enough, two lines showed up nice and dark pink.

"So, now what?"

"Now, you kiss your wife."

Micah kissed her soft and slow, and she melted into him as she always did when he kissed her like that. And then he held her while she cried, overcome and overwhelmed by the news that they had actually done it. They had made a baby together. They had beaten the odds that were so highly stacked against them.

"Thank you, Lord," Micah prayed softly.

"Thank you," Shannon echoed.

There were no odds so great that couldn't be conquered by faith, if God so willed it, and they were thankful a baby was His will for them.

Micah led her into the house for one more look before they joined the realtor outside. "What color should we paint the nursery?"

"Orange."

Micah's face screwed up. "Seriously? Like basketball orange? We don't even know if it's a boy."

"Girls play basketball, too, you know?"

"True."

"But I didn't mean basketballs. I meant paintball orange," she replied with a wink.

He laid a hand on her stomach. "No paint ball with the little one in there."

Her laughter echoed in the empty room. "We have time to figure it out."

When the doctor had told them their due date, Shannon couldn't help but picture God giving them a wink and a nod.

The tenth of June.

It was the anniversary of their first date, their wedding date, and now the date they would look forward to welcoming their little miracle.

Another June. And many more to come.

Acknowledgments

Thanks for reading Shannon and Micah's story. I spent quite a bit of time reading through people's journeys with PCOS and infertility. Having not dealt with either, I relied on the research to try to keep the story true to the struggle so many go through. I was touched by so many of the stories I read, all so different in how they dealt with it and what their outcome was. This being fiction, I wanted Shannon's story to have that happy ending, and that's the joy of writing. We can give our characters all the happiness we want for them. My prayers are with all the women who live with this diagnosis and other infertility issues.

My biggest thanks go out to my critique girls. They take time from their already busy author lives to read my books and help make them the best they can be for you. I couldn't do it without them.

I am blessed to have a wonderful group of readers, my launch team, who help spread the word about my books. Most have been with me since my first book, and they continue to get excited with me with each new release. Thanks, team!

Thanks to my husband for his unending love and support.

I loved starting this new series, and I'm excited to bring you the other McGregor siblings' stories. Very soon!

Happy reading, friends!
Krista

CPSIA information can be obtained
at www.ICGtesting.com
Printed in the USA
LVHW080203110319
610117LV00016BA/647/P